DATE DUE		

THE LIBRARY STORE   #47-0120

914.4   7538
Kim   Kimbrough, Emily,
         Floating island

Floating Island

Cando Community Library
Cando Library
Public Library

D0949771

Date Due

DEMCO NO. 294

DEC 6 '68	JUL 17 '78				
JAN 16 '69	AUG 03 '78				
FEB 8 '69	NOV 15 '78				
FEB 25 '69	FEB 7 '92				
MAR 21 '69					
MAY 21 '69					
NOV 4 '72					
JUL 8 '74					
FEB 25 '75					

FLOATING ISLAND

Books by
EMILY KIMBROUGH

OUR HEARTS WERE YOUNG AND GAY
with Cornelia Otis Skinner
WE FOLLOWED OUR HEARTS TO HOLLYWOOD
HOW DEAR TO MY HEART
. . . IT GIVES ME GREAT PLEASURE
THE INNOCENTS FROM INDIANA
THROUGH CHARLEY'S DOOR
FORTY PLUS AND FANCY FREE
SO NEAR AND YET SO FAR
WATER, WATER EVERYWHERE
AND A RIGHT GOOD CREW
PLEASURE BY THE BUSLOAD
FOREVER OLD, FOREVER NEW
FLOATING ISLAND

HARPER & ROW, PUBLISHERS
NEW YORK, EVANSTON, AND LONDON

44144
11-15-68
5.98

Emily Kimbrough Withdrawn

DRAWINGS BY MIRCEA VASILIU

FLOATING ISLAND

Withdrawn LIBRARY
Withdrawn
Devils Lake, N. Dak.

FLOATING ISLAND. *Copyright* © *1968 by Emily Kimbrough. Printed in the United States of America. All rights reserved. No part of this book may be used or reproduced in any manner whatsoever without written permission except in the case of brief quotations embodied in critical articles and reviews. For information address Harper & Row, Publishers, Incorporated, 49 East 33rd Street, New York, N.Y. 10016.*

FIRST EDITION

LIBRARY OF CONGRESS CATALOG CARD NUMBER: 68-15962

I-S

True happiness arises from the friendship and conversation of a few select companions. —Addison

To my select companions, Albert, Bobs, Brother, Emily, Frances, Margalo, Neill, Romney, Sam, and Sophy, with love.

FLOATING ISLAND

CABLE from London dated December 9th: "Parsons not known at Super Travel." It had been sent to my name and proper address in New York, but the communication itself was wrapped in fog. Super Travel did not know Parsons, but I had never heard of Super Travel. The cable I had sent on December 6th had been to Captain Richard Parsons, Continental Waterway Cruises, 169 Sloan Street, London, S.W.1. It read: "No reply urgent letter. Please cable collect."

The only part of the return message that seemed to answer my request was that it was sent to me collect. Two days later, when I had not cabled a reply because I was trying to reduce my bewilderment to a financially reasonable number of words, I received a letter from Super Travel Limited, 107 Walton Street, London, S.W.3.:

1

"Dear Miss Kimbrough: I am very sorry that you had to cable us but your letter was addressed to 169 Sloan Street and has only just reached us. I have pleasure in enclosing the provisional details for the 'Palinurus' for next season. The new brochure will be out at the beginning of January but I enclose a copy of last year's for your information." (In the next paragraph, having to do with available dates and routes, the writer suggested: "All this could be arranged at a later date with Richard Parsons.")

The letter ended: "I look forward to hearing from you, Yours sincerely, Diana Shirley."

Miss Shirley does not know how tepid was her invitation to further correspondence compared to the nearly hysterical eagerness of my acceptance. The correspondence grew; its bulk now fills a large file in my study, but I have never learned and I am reasonably sure I shall never know, how the "Continental Waterway Cruises" became "Super Travel Limited," that disclaimed knowledge of a Captain Richard Parsons, who by letter two days later was referred to as Richard. However, I know Diana Shirley: she is charming, eager, enthusiastic, vivacious. Efficiency is her goal, but she does not wish to arrive at it by means of tiresome minutiae. Richard, not Captain Parsons, is known to Diana Shirley and that should be enough for anybody.

Like every other trip I have made, this one was conceived long before it was accomplished. I am hazy about the specific date. It must have been sometime in November, because I was on a speaking tour in California where I had a letter from Sophy. For many years Sophy has been the indispensable companion of every sizable excursion I have ventured. The designation "companion" is inaccurate. "The General" is a title most frequently applied, and one to which she responds with a deprecatory modesty that would not fool a child. No one with whom I have traveled has ever thought to allow me that title. The only recognition I receive is a nod of acknowledgment that the idea for the trip was mine. From the moment my idea is accepted I am relegated to whatever position in the group is the lowest. This time, however, the positions were reversed. The idea for the trip was Sophy's and, for a short time after, I had the heady experience of executing it. My tenure of office was brief.

In the letter to me in California Sophy wrote she had been told of a converted barge in France owned and run by a young Englishman. From June to September he took individual passengers, but out of season the whole barge could be chartered for a cruise on French waterways. She suggested, "Why don't we gather a group of friends and take over the barge whenever it's available, perhaps in the spring?"

There was the idea sprung full panoplied from the General's brow. I embraced it with fervor and a telegram.

"Get all possible details. Home Thursday. Love."

There was no logical reason for the General to hand over to me the details she had accumulated. Perhaps we were both bewildered by the reversal of an established pattern. Perhaps the General wanted to sit back and savor the triumph of having had an idea. As a matter of fact, thinking back on it now I realize it was not such a reversal. Sophy gave me names, addresses and orders.

"This is where to reach Captain Parsons," she said. "Write him."

That letter, unanswered, and a following cable, introduced me to Miss Diana Shirley. We had scarcely begun to be pen pals, however, when a stranger came between us, one D. R. Lewthwaite by name, gender not disclosed. The letters themselves I found obscure. I shared them with Sophy. The first one began: "I am sorry about the confusion over the length of the cruise. It was a slip of mine, mentioning a ten-day holiday. I should of course have said twelve days, which is what we consider the period 29th of April to the 11th of May to be. Ship passengers join the boat on the evening of the 29th and leave on the morning of the 11th." (Our departure date was scheduled for April 27th.)

Next letter: "I am sorry you were confused by the choice mentioned on the booking form."

Following letter, and now Miss Shirley had come back to me: "Your confusion about the schedule for the *Palinurus* . . ."

Sophy looked up from her reading to make a suggestion: "Perhaps I had better take over the correspondence; you get the people." The old order was restored. I hope it will never be reversed again. I am not five-star material.

The assignment was easy for me. I had revealed my incompetence at business letters, either writing or understanding them; I am by nature a saleswoman. I have never sold Fuller brushes nor Avon beauty products, but I sold places on the *Palinurus* so rapidly the passenger list opened and closed the same day.

Alphabetically it read:

Romney Brent, actor, lecturer, teacher, director. Mexican by birth, he grew up in Paris. He needed only to be told the route would be in France, and who else was going. Congenial people on board and the sound of French ashore did not often happen, he said.

Margalo Gillmore, actress, author. The sound of French, she said, made her nervous, but to move slowly along quiet waterways—no high seas, not even waves—through beautiful country in the spring was irresistible.

Frances and Albert Hackett, playwrights. They love travel. This was transportation they had never used. The variety offered appealed to them too, when I told them bicycles were carried on board for pleasure and exercise on the towpath between locks.

Sophia Yarnall Jacobs, distinguished in the fields of civil rights and race relations, did not have to be sold. It was her idea.

Emily and Charles Kimbrough, my brother and sister-in-law (duplication of names confusing), did not have to be sold. Hearing about the trip they invited themselves. My sister-in-law had never been abroad, Brother longed to return to France.

Rear Admiral Neill Phillips (Ret.) was pleased by the prospect of a barge. It would be a change.

Cornelia Otis Skinner, actress and author, volunteered her participation. Her knowledge of French, she affirmed, would be invaluable. Though she, Sophy and I have been close friends for more years than we would dream of stating, I should not have mentioned to the General, Cornelia's self-evaluation. The General derives satisfaction from her own skill in the language.

Dr. Samuel Standard, a distinguished surgeon and teacher, recently retired. For many years he had been a well-known figure in the section of New York through which he rode his bicycle daily between his apartment and his hospital. He was delighted to be offered another route, and his favorite vehicle. It seemed to me a roundabout way to achieve a bicycle route. Dr. Sam defended it, mentioning as an afterthought he had only been in Europe once before, a three-hour stopover in Paris on his way to Israel. He had gone from the airport to the Rodin Museum and back again. Two weeks on rivers and canals in France would undoubtedly provide a wider vista.

CARNEGIE LIBRARY
Devils Lake, N. Dak.

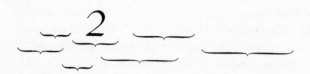

2

GEOGRAPHIC details and time schedules were placed in the hands of the General, but there were consultations among the women about what clothes to take. Cornelia insisted this was more difficult for her than for any of us. In the opinion of her friends Cornelia dresses extremely well, with flair and an acute perception of what is smart for her. To assure her of this makes very little impression. She is of a mournful conviction her clothes and the occasions for wearing them are never in harmony but together form a mean and deliberate conspiracy against her.

"You have a clothes problem?" I suggested.

To know her for any length of time is to realize that, although she does not allow herself to be swamped by them, little problems and little plans are a not inconsiderable frac-

tion of her daily pattern. When reminded of this characteristic she sometimes turns a bit testy. This was one of the
times. She actually tossed her head.

"All right, all right," she said. "Perhaps you think this
nothing at all." She enumerated on her fingers. "I am going
from the barge trip to Paris, from there to Italy, after that on
a North Cape cruise and then to London. I suppose you are
aware each of these places has a separate climate and will,
of course, include separate activities. I'll have to pack the
clothes for each trip in a separate bag."

The pessimism that envelops when she is beset by problems came upon her. "I will undoubtedly arrive on the barge
with a wardrobe for dining and theatregoing in London. I
will reach Italy with sweaters and padded robes for the
frozen North and be equipped to sweep down to dinner at
the Savoy in slacks and sweater."

We gave her the sympathy we assured her was deserved. We
shared her melancholy about her possible apparel in London
because the six women of the group were facing dismally the
unavoidable purchase of slacks. Age with its inevitable devel-
opments precluded the chance of their becoming us.

Always on boats we said there are knobs or things of a sort
that stick out—we did not ask the Admiral to define them—
whatever made them necessary in the construction of a boat
made them also traps for catching skirts. Slacks must be borne.
However, we would take along dresses to wear when we
went sightseeing, out of deference to the sensibilities of the
local citizenry. We are critical, we agreed, of American women
who at home scrupulously conform to the standards of ap-
propriateness, but traveling abroad will dress with bland in-
difference to the conventions of the country, evidently on the
assumption they are unlikely to meet anyone they know and
therefore it doesn't matter.

The mournful consensus of opinion, too, was that undoubtedly it would rain every day and be very cold. We must take warm clothes and all possible storm protection, from boots to rain hats.

Frances led the way in the purchase of slacks. She gave the rest of us not only the name of the shop but the name of the saleswoman.

"Do go to her," she urged. "She is so kind. Albert was with me and before I came out of the dressing room to show him how I looked, she went ahead of me. He told me afterward she leaned over him and said, 'Now you are not to laugh.' "

Frances was the leader, too, in a trial bicycle spin in Central Park. It was her suggestion, "Just to get the feel of it again." Margalo and Cornelia withdrew at the last minute, offering frail excuses, but Sophy and I followed Frances on a Sunday morning with Albert in general attendance and insistence on treating us to the ride.

The morning was warm and sunny. The park is a lovely sight on weekend days when all automobile traffic is prohibited; like a Breughel in animation and variety of color. Though we said to one another how much we appreciated the animation and variety of color, we were a little dismayed and considerably intimidated by the crowd of bicycles producing it. Except in Holland I have never seen so many at the same time. Even our leader faltered at the sight. But Frances is not one to abandon a plan, particularly one she has promoted.

"Perhaps there won't be any bicycles left to rent," she suggested, "but we'll have to ask."

There were bicycles available though not the kind I requested when my turn came. To my astonishment my request mortified the others, Sophy said. I had asked the man allotting them if it would be possible to adjust to the size model I would require, a set of training wheels—that extra small pair I have seen attached one on either side of the rear wheel to prevent children from tipping over when they are learning to ride.

"I am not learning," I had explained, "but I could tip over very easily."

The attachment, the man explained, would not fit an adult bicycle. I was sorry to learn this. I had made up my mind on the instant of requesting them to order a pair, have it shipped over to the barge, and put on whatever model I would ride there. Sophy said she thanked a merciful Providence this would not be possible, and that surprised me.

Across a path from the rental bureau we discovered a wide circular open space, probably on weekdays a parking area for cars. We wheeled our vehicles to it immediately, not needing to say aloud each had marked this as a sheltered, untraveled spot for practice. I was not surprised to see Albert fling a leg over the bar, catch the opposite pedal and sprint off, curving at the turns with exact calculation. I was not so surprised as irritated to see Sophy after a few wobbles follow him with assurance. I was delighted to find myself, after a few more wobbles and at a slower pace, following them; but rounding a curve I was flabbergasted to see Frances.

At the moment of my departure she had been standing astride her cycle, one foot on the far pedal the other on the ground, and as I passed her she had said, "I can't get up the nerve to take my foot off the ground."

What I saw was Frances, a foot on each pedal, moving straight out of our nursery area into the stream of bicycle traffic, all of it one way. She was heading into it, a lone figure going upstream. The next instant she was out of my sight, engulfed. Albert passed me and I called after him: "Frances has more nerve than any of us. She's gone out."

"My God," was his answer. "Which way?"

Certainly I could not take a hand off a handlebar to point but I nodded in the direction I had last seen her.

Before my next curve came, I saw Albert cut across and through the bicycle river to the far side. Some time later, when exhaustion and leg ache had given me the nerve to jump off my wheel, I saw Frances returning. Albert was riding close behind her, not unlike a sheep dog, nudging at her back wheel, and holding her to the side of the road. They came into our private race track, Frances heading straight for a bank that was its boundary.

"I don't know how to stop," she explained as I scrambled out of her way. "I'll have to fall." She slowed until the bicycle, from lack of motion, toppled over and Frances with it, on the bank, so gently neither she nor the machine was harmed. A police car driving in at some speed came to a stop beside her and a young officer jumped out. Standing above her as she lay on the bank, he asked if she were hurt. When she assured him she was not in the least, he wiped his forehead with a handkerchief.

"Well, lady," he told her, "all I can say is the way you ride you ought to wear a helmet."

When the car had gone and Albert had removed the bicycle, helping Frances leave the bank, I told her my admiration for her courage, her impatience with sissy practice in empty spaces. She looked surprised.

"Why," she said, "I went out there because I had to. I don't know how to turn. It was hell. But I knew Albert would find me."

Albert was like the policeman. He took out a handkerchief and wiped his forehead.

I asked if they had seen Sophy.

"Out there," Albert indicated. "She passed us, but she's with the traffic."

I was sorry I had asked. I might have known this would happen. I was the one, as usual, at the post. Now I wish I had been resigned to that. It is my habitual place in any group engaged in activity, and I have passed the age of feeling obliged to be a good or any kind of sport. Nevertheless, illogically, I headed my wheel toward the exit.

"I think I'll follow Sophy," I told the Hacketts. I must have been demented. As I pedaled slowly and unsteadily past them I heard Frances say, "I'm going to stay beside this bank and practice falling off."

On the instant of leaving our dear sequestered grove I knew my heart was back where the Hacketts were, such part of it as was not pounding in my throat and perhaps the cause of my legs trembling like poplar leaves in a breeze. Getting into the stream of life around me had not been difficult. I had simply closed my eyes as I moved out of our sanctuary. Opening them had brought on the tremors. All the bicycles except mine were going fast, their drivers exhibiting a shocking disregard for the courtesy of passing only on the left. I was passed on either side with bells squawking at me and rude shouts sent back. At its peak my strength is far below the strength of ten, and, unlike Sir Galahad's too, what of it I have is not due to a purity of heart. Indignation, however, will arouse it and fury at least double it. The bells, the shouting, and the passing drove my feet down hard on the pedals. My legs, sturdy as oak limbs now, churned in splendid rhythm until they brought me to a hill, not much of a hill. I had walked with my dog along that road and not been aware it sloped; but having both feet on the ground is not the same as pushing them on pedals. I pushed, panted, accomplishing now a speed that scarcely kept the vehicle upright.

A fresh chorus of shouts to get a move on is undoubtedly what injected the adrenalin that brought me to the summit and over the crest. The breeze sang in my ears as I began the down coast. I think I even sang a little myself, but the breeze seemed to change to an ominous whistle I did not care for. When I became aware I was the one passing other cyclists I

became increasingly alarmed. With neither the desire nor the ability to turn my head, I had not looked at the landscape, but, daring a swift sideways glance, I knew my suspicions were founded on fact. The landscape was blurred by the speed at which I was passing it. When I caught up with and whizzed through a racing club—I suppose that is what it was; I caught a blur of striped sweaters and bodies horizontal over drooping handlebars—I had no doubt I was far beyond myself and, in the words of the old hymn, "Nearer My God to Thee." Brakes were what were needed, and they were on the handlebars; so were my hands, only a few inches away, but so deeply embedded by fright it seemed beyond my strength to disinter them. I know now that desperation is as good as anger for developing bodily strength. I got my hands off, up, and around the brakes and I squeezed with all my new might.

This accomplishment was only a trivial curtain raiser to the feature production that followed. I have seen in vaudeville and circus acts a bicyclist, putting his head on the handlebars, slowly and delicately elevate his body until, legs together, feet pointed up, he travels straight as an arrow, upside down. My body did not go up in the air delicately, nor did my feet point toward the sky, but my rear, all of it, loomed above my head, my lower limbs remaining in a pedaling position well above the pedals. Had I been given a choice, I would unhesitatingly have asked to go all the way over the handlebars, with the machine on me, and lie unconscious while an ambulance came and mercifully removed me. I was not so favored. After a lifetime of suspension upended I was back in the saddle again with an uncomfortable impact.

I heard a child's voice say, "Daddy, did you see *that?*"

Humiliation, I think, never touches bottom. Sophy was among the spectators. She came from behind me calling, "Are you all right?" As idiotic an inquiry as I ever heard.

"Certainly," I told her. Perhaps my voice sounded a little uneven, "I was just going too fast, that's all."

She rode beside me. "I think you must have put on both brakes at once," she suggested, "and maybe a little too hard. You ought to use only one at a time."

I did not consider this an appropriate moment for education. I made no answer.

"Would you like me to go back with you?" she offered. "I'm ready to turn in. I'm tired."

I thanked her but said I thought I would not go in just yet.

"I'm a little tired too," I said, "but I think I'll sit on the grass a few minutes and watch. You go on."

I had no intention of getting off while she was there, to let her see my legs had turned to poplar leaves again. "That's quite a hill to come up, back there, isn't it?"

"What hill?" she echoed. Taking one hand away, the showoff, she pointed to a contraption I had not noticed under my handlebars.

"Why," she said, "you're in high speed. I don't see how you could get up any slope. Didn't you know that?"

Something must have told her I wanted to be alone.

"We'll meet back at our place," she called, riding off.

When I dismounted, my legs, as I had anticipated, caved in under me. When they let me up again I walked my wheel to our rendezvous; it did not seem much of a walk. We turned in our bicycles, and that was the last time Frances and I rode.

3

BY early April the company of eleven was well into the last lap of preparation. Passports were in order, all vaccinations verified or taken. In a Sunday telephone call Brother told me his had taken so violently he had wondered at about three o'clock one morning if the trip was really worth it. He had been more confused than mollified by his wife's words of comfort, when she told him this ought to make him doubly appreciative of the trip, otherwise he wouldn't have known how vulnerable he was. A speaking date in Chicago gave me an opportunity to spend a night with them. I was shown Brother's new camera, but I was more edified by their dining in sneakers; to get used to the feeling of them, they explained, since neither had worn flat soles for years.

"I wear my raincoat and hat in the house quite a lot too,"

my sister-in-law explained. "I don't want them to look new."
She is somewhat given to obscure observations.

  They would fly directly to London, they told me. Sophy,
the Hacketts and I had the same plan. Margalo, Romney and
Neill were going direct to Paris. Sam and Cornelia would
leave earlier than any of us, traveling on the *Queen Mary*
to Cherbourg. A suggestion from the travel bureau did not
seem feasible—that we all come from Paris and be met at
Fontainebleau by Captain Parsons. Why should those of us
flying from London go into Paris and then out again? Why
not hire a car at Orly and come direct, letting the others
decide their own transportation from Paris? This proposal
seemed agreeable to the Chicago Kimbroughs, and also that
Sophy and I would engage a room for them at the Carlton
Tower in London, where we would be staying. The Kimbroughs' arrival there would be a day ahead of ours. The
Hacketts would be ahead of all of us in London.

  Cornelia, Sophy and I had supper together the Sunday
night after my return from Chicago. Cornelia seemed pre-
occupied, I thought, and I was not mistaken. Midway in the
meal she interrupted something Sophy was saying.

  "There's one aspect of the trip," she said, "that does not
seem feasible to me. In fact, I think it is quite a problem."

  Sophy, a little annoyed at being interrupted, was snappish.
"You and your little problems," she said.

  Cornelia smiled. "I think you'll share this one," was her
acid reply. "Now," she continued, "the travel bureau says we
will board the *Palinurus* at Fontainebleau?"

  Sophy acknowledged this.

  "Where, may I ask, will we find a barge, any boat in
Fontainebleau? Perhaps you know a hidden river but the
only body of water I know is the pond by the château where
you can feed those bloated and disgusting carp."

  The pause that followed was dramatic without Cornelia's

help. The General broke it. Her face was red but she is a magnanimous woman.

"I ought to soak my head in that pond," she said. "How could I have been such a fool? Of course there's no waterway in Fontainebleau. There are other things I don't know, too, such as where we're going after we do not leave from Fontainebleau."

She brought from the correspondence file a letter from the Super Travel Agency.

"This is an answer I had to my request for the specific route." She read aloud:

" 'Dear Mrs. Jacobs, Thank you for your letter. I wrote to you on thirtieth March with the day-to-day itinerary and a letter from Richard Parsons. I am very sorry that this has not arrived and I cannot understand why, as we sent it airmail.

" 'I'm afraid we can do very little now as Richard Parsons did a special itinerary for you and I am afraid I did not make a copy of it. I cannot contact him. He has returned to France. The best I can do is give you the following from memory. I think it is fairly accurate. . . .'

"I'll ask about Fontainebleau," Sophy said when she had finished reading. "I hope Miss Shirley will remember our starting place." She was nettled, and admitted it.

"I can't imagine why I've been accepting Fontainebleau all along. Of course, there's no river there nor canal. There can't be another Fontainebleau, at least I've never heard of it." The General prides herself on her map-reading ability and geographic knowledge.

Her irritation had noticeably lessened when she repeated to me the following morning a telephone conversation with the Plaza Travel Service in New York.

"They've engaged a car and driver. Thank God for their efficiency. We'll be met at Orly and taken to," she paused, "I had to say Fontainebleau. I felt such a fool trying to explain that I would have to let them know later where we were really going. It's going to cost us $75. That seems an awful lot, but divided among the Hacketts, the other Kimbroughs, you and me it won't be so bad."

It was not bad. In the end the ride cost us nothing at all, because five days before our takeoff for London I was offered the use of a Volkswagen Microbus. This is a vehicle dear to my heart. A Microbus carried four companions and me through the valleys and without a gasp, except from me, over the mountains of Portugal. I would have welcomed the car out of reminiscent sentiment alone, but in accepting it with many thanks I was also following a principle I set down years ago: Accept gracefully anything that is offered, and think afterward what to do with it.

Sophy mentioned this functional aspect when I told her gleefully the beautiful manna that had dropped on us. "Where on earth will we put it?" Amplifying, "You can't stow it on the barge nor tow it behind. Will somebody have to drive it along the nearest road? It's certainly too big to go on a tow-path."

"That's the best part of it," was my answer. "It's big enough to hold all of us at one time; that is, if two sit in the luggage part in the rear and face each other. We can take turns."

Sophy thought this recommendation irrelevant; but when I told her she would, of course, do the driving, a function established in Portugal, she brightened visibly. When I reminded her since the Microbus would meet us at Orly we could cancel the $75 car, she was even commendatory. We decided to keep the acquisition a surprise for the others, at least until we had worked out a way of using it beyond the trip from Orly to Fontainebleau or wherever.

In Sophy's mail on the morning of April 21st—one day before she and I would fly to London—there were two letters.

One was from Miss Shirley, the other was the one from Captain Richard Parsons to which Miss Shirley referred in the letter Sophy had read aloud to Cornelia and me. It had indeed been sent on March 30th but not by air. It contained the full and explicit day-to-day itinerary. Miss Shirley's memory had not been photographic.

To spread this new knowledge was not easy. Cornelia and Dr. Standard were somewhere in the Atlantic on the *Queen Mary*. Frances and Albert were in London, Margalo, Romney still in New York and Neill in Virginia. The Chicago Kimbroughs were poised for flight. A copy of the mistaken route had been given every member before his departure, so that addresses for sending and forwarding mail could be established.

Copies of the revised route were frantically typed and dispatched to as many as we could reach. It had to be given by telephone to Chicago since that departure was so imminent. Happily no change was needed from the place and time of our first rendezvous. This had been agreed before the exodus had begun: 1 P.M., April 27th. Café L'Aigle Noir, Fontainebleau.

The point of embarkation was correctly given on Captain Parsons' itinerary. A fuller description came from Miss Shirley. I shall keep her letter in my memory book.

It reads: ". . . Actually, the barge will not be at Fontainebleau, but at a place called Samois only about five kilometers away. Samois is a small place and the barge will be moored on the river by the Café Fernand."

The sentence that follows deserves a place among the great utterances in the English language: "I am told you cannot help missing it."

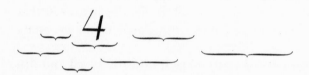

4

AT ten o'clock on the morning of April 27th, three Kimbroughs, two Hacketts and Sophy, together with a planeload of other passengers, arrived at Orly, at the end of something under an hour's flight from London. The day may come when I will consider of no interest to anyone the news that I boarded a plane and walked off it at the anticipated destination. I shall have to live a very long time for this to happen. I daresay Mr. Rusk does not enliven a Cabinet meeting with the jubilant announcement, "Look, fellows, I flew from London yesterday and here I am." I say, however, we flew from London and there we were at Orly.

Porters brought our luggage to a spot they seemed to recognize as a boundary, said we must get others to take it further, and left. Brother went outside with Sophy to see if a

Volkswagen Microbus could be actually waiting for us. Albert went to find porters. After a few minutes with me, Frances went off to find Albert. From my post beside the luggage I gave information to my sister-in-law, who, some distance away, was standing in an area that seemed to have no purpose, objects of interest, newsstand, customs or whatever.

"Don't look for Brother," I called. "He's gone with Sophy."

"I know," was her answer. "I'm just listening to people going by, speaking French. Isn't it beautiful?" With a grin she acknowledged her own idiocy: "They speak it so well."

Albert returned with porters, without Frances. Brother came in with the news that our Microbus was waiting, and Sophy already at the wheel. Emily was coaxed away by a promise of French to be heard in other places, and the luggage was carried out. While I was thanking the gentleman who had brought the car, receiving his card so that I might telephone him when we were ready to turn it back, Frances joined us. She was breathless and a little cross with Albert for not having been where she could find him, but the sight of the Volkswagen and the General in her place distracted and delighted her. We rolled away.

Since we were early for the appointed rendezvous at the restaurant L'Aigle Noir in Fontainebleau we did not pause there but went straight on, following, after one wrong turn, the signs to Samois, and Sophy was not displeased by the error because she was the first to recognize it. Another sign impossible to be passed unnoticed made us wince uncomfortably. We caught sight of it simultaneously. Across a wall in straggling large letters of black paint we read, "Johnson l'Assassin." Sophy paused involuntarily at the shock of seeing it.

No one spoke at the moment but when we had moved on

Frances said, "Well, it's not as if that was unexpected. We've all been told this is the kind of thing we'll find. So it's just as well I suppose to see it early and be braced for it."

It was a futile bracing. We did not see another sign of its kind in any part of the France we traveled, nor did we receive anything but cordiality and friendliness from the French people we encountered, and we encountered many.

Samois is a charming little town, I think. We did not explore it. We had a single objective. We found the Seine without difficulty since the main road runs beside it. We saw the Café Fernand, but no boat of any kind moored to the bank. Because there was no place there to turn around, we continued along the road and at the end of perhaps half a mile saw lying low in the water what we knew by its shape to be a barge. Unmistakably there was our home away from home, the *Palinurus,* tantalizingly out of our reach. No wonder, with all of us shouting the discovery, Sophy became impetuous. I hope the householder's shrubbery into which she backed was not irreparably damaged, but we were turned around and headed the way we had come in a remarkably swift maneuver. At the point of entrance to this road we found on our return a bridge and beyond it a footpath. Deciding among us it would be less formidable than the full group, if emissaries went, Brother and I followed the path, leaving the others in the car. We had almost reached the barge when a young man jumped from it to the bank and came toward us smiling, hand outstretched.

"I am Captain Richard Parsons," he said. "Are you Miss Kimbrough?" We shook hands.

We had been told the Captain was a young man but I had not anticipated one quite so youthful; in his twenties, I thought, and learned later he was twenty-seven. I thought, too, how endearingly young it was to tell us his title with pride, and perhaps a little anxiety for immediate recognition.

Like a mind reader at that instant turning to me he added, smiling shyly, "I'm called Richard."

He had been telling Brother politely, but with not very well-concealed dismay, he had not expected us until four o'clock in the afternoon. He had understood that hour for embarkation had been made clear in the correspondence. I assured him it had indeed been made very clear. (I could have told him a few things in the correspondence that had not been of such crystal clarity.) We had not thought to come on board, I said, but arriving early for our lunch appointment in Fontainebleau, had driven on, eager to see the barge and, if it were possible, stow our luggage. We would not return with the others until four o'clock. Reassured, he invited us to come aboard though he hoped we would excuse the untidiness.

He led the way up a short flight of steps, steep as a stile. With his considerable help and a boost behind from Brother I was hoisted from the top step over a rim and onto the deck. I knew, then, with grim certainty, for the next two weeks I would be wearing slacks. Ducking our heads by instruction from the Captain, we went through a door to a small landing. Three steps down on either side of it led to a long room we would know later and enjoy. At the moment I was aware only of general confusion, chairs upended on top of one another, and, at the far end, three young women, rather grubby, a little shy, but welcoming. We were introduced to Jennifer, small with dark hair falling on one side of her face, pushed behind her ear on the other side.

"Jennifer is the housekeeper, stewardess, general caretaker," Captain Richard explained, "and Emma is barmaid and chef's assistant."

Emma was blonde, hair "teased" high on her head. This and the miniskirt she wore, the shortest until then I had seen, probably made her look taller, I thought, than she actually was. Later when I knew her better I realized had her hair been as flat to her head as Jennifer's and her skirts ankle length she still would have grazed the ceiling of the saloon; she was a tall girl. The third young woman, of a height between Jennifer's and Emma's, hair not so blonde as Emma's, was the Captain's fiancée, he told us. On a few days' holiday visit to the *Palinurus,* she would soon be returning to her job in London.

Brother was acknowledging the introductions and shaking hands with each of the girls when I saw his eyes widen. He was facing me; whatever caused this look was coming in from the deck behind us.

"Oh," Jennifer said, "and this is my husband David." Before I turned to meet the arrival I saw Brother's lips move. Later, questioned, Brother told me fervently, "The hand of the Lord must have been clapped over my mouth at that moment. I thought it was some Frenchman doing work on the boat. I was just about to say in English so he wouldn't understand, 'And this is John the Baptist.' The second between was split when Jennifer said, 'And this is my husband David.' "

David is no more French than the Midlands in England from which he comes. He chooses to wear a magnificent Biblical curly, luxuriant beard that narrows only a little when it reaches his ears; a genial smile runs through it. He was the engineer, the Captain told us, as well as Jennifer's husband of six months.

On the *Palinurus* he would be the pilot too, and general mechanic. He had heard Brother's and my request to put our luggage on board and had come to suggest he with the Captain row back in the dinghy as near as possible to our car, stow the luggage there and row it to the barge. To walk the path heavily burdened had not been a happy prospect.

Before we left, we were shown the cabins. The way to them was down a short flight of stairs immediately under the landing from the deck. Brother, neglecting to duck, rapped his forehead smartly against the sharp edge of the landing that was also the overhead of the stairway down. Brother said the cabins looked very nice. He was pressing the palm of his hand against his forehead. Compared with what I had expected and experienced on the English canals, where we had occupied cells and slept on the equivalent of ironing boards,* these cabins seemed equivalent to accommodations on the *Queen Elizabeth*.

When we left the *Palinurus* I followed the Captain and preceded Brother. A sharp crack, an expletive in a high treble told me without looking back Brother had forgotten again to duck. When I offered sympathy he glared.

"I'm either going to develop a permanent stoop," he said, "and turn into a troll, or become an idiot from repeated brain injuries."

He made no further conversation the length of the path. The Captain and I talked and waved to bearded David in the dinghy.

Brother must have been as startled as I by the sight in the distance of a number of people surrounding our little group. He broke off the misanthropic predictions about his future, to ask if I thought we were being visited by a local delegation. I thought it more likely to be the other members of our own troupe I told him, and we hurried to meet them. They were as surprised as we and a touch discomfited to find our contingent had had the ingenuity to find the barge before lunch. Each had thought to be the ones to tell the others about it. Somewhere in the babel the Captain was introduced to everyone and to the combined accumulated luggage. I do

* *And a Right Good Crew.*

not know which was the more overwhelming, eleven people all talking at once to one another and to him or the size of the mound of luggage. It reminded me of the burial mound at Marathon that is said to entomb 192 soldiers. I do not know what the Captain thought of, looking at it. When we left he was discussing with David how many trips in the dinghy would be required.

The limousine that had brought the others from Paris was parked behind our Volkswagen. The contrast between them was noticeable. We had kept a secret the loan of the Microbus. The limousine set assumed this was the car we had hired to bring us from Orly. Learning it was ours for the duration provoked cries of surprise that bordered on the hysterical. "How wonderful." "Is it amphibious?" "How will we all fit?" The limousine was dismissed.

Albert and Romney solved the problem of accommodations by volunteering to sit on the floor behind the third tier of seats. They climbed up and in from the back, supervised by the General, who instructed them to cross their legs tailor fashion and face each other. Since she must close the back window, they could not dangle. This provoked expostulations and small cries of protest from Frances. Albert, she said, too closely confined would suffocate; she did not mention Romney. His reassurances, however, coupled with Albert's wordless snorts of indignation, persuaded her, though she affirmed she would keep an eye on him lest he begin to nod in stupor. Sophy, displaying her knowledge of tactics that has gone toward earning her the title of General, distracted Frances from this preoccupation by insisting she share the driver's seat. Sophy knew the ascent to this position is not easy. A Microbus rises high above the ground. To reach the front seat requires something between a leap and a clamber. Frances was not prepared for this and made several tries, hitching her skirt a little higher at each attempt. Trying futilely to help, I murmured as she sank back the second time, "Slacks are inevitable."

She nodded grimly, gave another hoist and clambered.

We retraced our way, passing once more the horrid sign to Americans. In Fontainebleau we went unerringly to the restaurant L'Aigle Noir. The proprietor was waiting; the reservations were in order. Yes, he assured us they had been made some time previously; again Sophy and I blessed the beautiful Plaza Travel Service in New York. He suggested we first have drinks in the bar. It was a happy choice for a send-off. In the overall *tohubohu* at Samois, individuals had not been sorted out. There were introductions to be made because each member did not know all the others. Some had not known Neill, others had never met my brother and sister-in-law. Presenting *them,* I said, presented a problem for the group. My sister-in-law's name, I told those who did not know her, is Emily.

"She is Emily Kimbrough like me. I don't know which is the more legitimate, hers by marriage, mine for keeping my unmarried name professionally; but there it is. Two Emily Kimbroughs. You'll have to work it out yourselves since obviously the hurdle to first names must be got over immediately. I have one suggestion that is perhaps a little nauseating. My brother's name is Charles but he is known and has always been known to my friends as well as in the family as Brother. His own wife frequently and absent-mindedly calls him Brother, incestuous as it may sound. Equally in the family I am known as Sister. We will therefore answer to Brother and Sister Kimbrough, unless you feel it carries the rather sickening taint of a revival meeting."

Cornelia broke in. "You might as well, while you're making a speech, tell the worst about me too."

I obliged. "Cornelia is known to her old friends as Bobs. She dislikes it but answers to it. It is too late now for Sophy

and me to change. I've tried calling her Cornelia. This only agitates her into a conviction I am offended at something. So make your choice. It's not easy. She's a delicate plant."

We visited the château immediately after lunch. It is directly across the road from the restaurant, and we fed the bloated carp.

At half past three (for the last hour I had been looking surreptitiously at my watch, and caught others doing the same thing) Neill said loudly, "I think we can get going now."

We were on our way.

5

THE interior of the *Palinurus* that afternoon at four o'clock was so changed as to make Brother and me stare at it and at each other. Every table and chair was in place and the long room was charming. Brother bumped his head going into it. Seeing Neill duck—and Neill was considerably the tallest of the eleven—he muttered accusingly, "Taught by submarines probably."

The Captain was explaining the room to the others. "This is the combined living and dining saloon and bar."

The bar was at the far end from where we stood at the bow. It consisted of a counter with what seemed to be well-stocked shelves behind and three high stools in front.

"Emma is the barmaid; you'll meet her a little later. She will fill your orders and make up your separate chits."

Something about his manner, we agreed later, made us realize at once there would be no informality about this procedure, no casual stepping behind the bar on our part to fix a drink and make a note of it. The young captain was making it clear at the outset his ship would be run properly and with authority.

"Breakfast," he continued, "is between eight and nine. The tables are separate then, so you can make any groups you choose or eat alone. For lunch and dinner they are combined into one. Luncheon will be at one, dinner at eight." He smiled diffidently. "If it is agreeable to all of you I should like to invite the crew and myself to dine with you tonight; after that we will eat separately."

A number of voices assured him it would indeed be agreeable.

"Your stewardess—her name is Jennifer—will show you your cabins now if you like."

Again he was observing convention. A captain does not show the staterooms to his passengers.

Jennifer, the small dark-haired girl I had met before, was waiting at the foot of the short flight of stairs under the landing. Family pride makes me reluctant to note that on the way down Brother cracked his head. He continued to accomplish this with monotonous regularity until two or perhaps three days later. Evidently, acknowledging finally his inability to remember and anticipate the low landmarks, he chose the less dangerous alternative. Most of the time when he moved about indoors, he curved and bent himself into his threatened facsimile of a troll.

My impression of the room we were quitting that day was that it seemed light, adequately large and comfortable. I had no reason to change my first impression and like the others came to know the room very well. I found it had eight double windows on either side, and at the bow end two windows and a door on the landing that opened to the forward deck, where there would be armchairs, deckchairs and, when the warm weather recommended, beach umbrellas. These would be set in holes that had been made through the centers of closed barrels, painted black with a red stripe. They also served as small tables. Under the windows at the bow end of the saloon I later discovered bookshelves and made a contribution to the library they contained when I left behind at the end of the cruise the detective stories I had purchased in London. Sam Standard, however, was to discover and claim for his own, by endeavoring to memorize parts of it, an extraordinary volume. I never learned how it came to be there. It was entitled *Voir la Mer*, published around the middle of the nineteenth century. Sam committed bits of this to memory. He hoped to deliver one of these, he said, as an opening flourish perhaps to a shopkeeper with whom he wished to effect a transaction. It would supplement the knowledge of the language with which he had come; at a generous count, I would have put it at twenty words. I never heard one of these preliminaries but I like to conjure up an image of the expression on a shopkeeper's face when Sam, after a conventional *"Bonjour,"* may have told him, and I translate literally, "The sea is the dream of every townsman or countryman however small his curiosity may be toward the grand scenes of nature."

On this first inspection of the room we did not come upon Sam's gold mine. We looked at and approved low comfortable armchairs, with tables between, along one side of the saloon, their backs against the windows as if one were sitting on a bus. Opposite these, the tables the Captain had previously indicated were set against the wall, like end tables. Each would accommodate three people comfortably, one at the end, one on either side. Incidental as these were to the overall arrangements of the barge, more than any other detail of our accommodations they made possible the one thing we had thought we must sacrifice in such close quarters, privacy. Had the long dining table been a fixture, we would have sat at it only at mealtime, but these movable pieces, we learned in the first twenty-four hours, permitted the one who liked to be alone with his breakfast coffee, bracing himself for the day and its demands, to seat himself at an unoccupied table. Those rare ones who enjoyed jollity with their croissants could find companions. During the rest of the day the same effortless privacy was accomplished. Unless we were all off on an excursion there was not a time when the room was empty.

On that first day's cursory appraisal we were more impressed and agreeably surprised by the cabins. Except for two rooms in the stern, each was furnished with a double bed, and in addition a bedside table with shelves, a chair, an ample closet and a washstand. Sophy and I took the ones on either side of the main corridor at the bow, thinking we were being unselfishly accommodating, because they were the farthest from the baths. They turned out to be the largest. Margalo settled in next to Sophy, and Cornelia just beyond. On my side of the corridor Emily came next. We allotted the two beyond to Neill and Sam because they were the biggest men and these were the biggest beds. This left an unoccupied one next to Cornelia. Sophy and I, taking charge, assigned this for storing all the luggage when it had been unpacked.

From the time of the early planning of the trip Frances and Albert had requested a double cabin with twin beds, but an inspection of the two on the barge brought about a reluctant change of mind. Each of these did include two beds but they were bunks, narrow, placed at right angles and one above the other, at such a height as to allow scant clearance for the feet of the person in the lower bunk and to make it impossible for the occupant of the upper one to sit up without cracking his head on the ceiling. Frances took one of these double rooms, conceding that perhaps Albert had better take the single next door. He did, and cracked his head every morning against the low ceiling. He told me it probably felt the same as the one in the double cabin, but he did not tell Frances this. A duplicate arrangement on the opposite side gave Brother, by the toss of a coin, the double and Romney the single. Romney, shorter than Albert but with a longer memory, received no head injury. Brother, also warned by Albert, rolled out of bed without sitting up, and immediately assumed his daily curvature. On their side also and toward the center (amidships I daresay is the proper term) were a shower, a tub and a W.C. On Frances's and Albert's side a shower and a W.C.

We did not learn that day the hazards that would make bathing an adventure, but Jennifer immediately gave an illustrated lecture on operating the W.C. The long handle extending from the wall was for flushing, accomplished by pumping. Pumping, to be successful, must be exercised when the lid of the W.C. was tightly closed. The best way of insuring this was by pressing it down with the knee. You could hold it down with one hand, she said, while you pumped with the other, but this meant both stooping down and reaching up, dissipating one's strength. The best way was to stand up on one foot, press down the lid with the opposite knee and pull the pump handle. She invited us to try. We were happy to oblige but incompetent, confused between pumping and pressing. All of us except Brother. He immediately caught the knack and the distribution required. He was modest about his superiority and generous about putting it to service.

During several days after, a call would go out: "Find Brother and ask him to man the pump." He gave himself the inaccurate but phonetic title of "Monsieur le Pompier."

The demonstration completed the tour and we scattered to

unpack. At seven o'clock we were assembled in the saloon for drinks.

Captain Richard joined us but did not take a drink. He wanted to explain a few things to everyone, he said, and to talk particularly with Sophy and me. He was scowling a little and gave an ominous appearance of having something unpleasant to say and wanting to get it over. He was not happy, he said, about the news that I had been loaned a Volkswagen Microbus. Where would this car be kept? How would we get it to the boat, since he would be unable to tell in advance where he would be at a given time? He had no way of knowing, since it would depend entirely on the amount of traffic, whether we would go into and out of a lock immediately we reached it, or be held back by others ahead of us for perhaps an hour, perhaps three or four. He found himself obliged to urge us to leave the car at Samois in the garage whose proprietor he knew. At the end of a week we should be at Auxerre, where we would stop for a full day and night. This would allow time to hire another car to take us back to Samois, pick up the Volkswagen and perhaps use it during the last week, when we would have left the rivers for the Burgundy Canal, and where traffic would be much lighter. Furthermore, this would be the part of the countryside providing interesting places to visit. He hoped we would accept this proposal. Any other way he was sure would be disrupting.

Sophy gave me a look of commiseration, a little tinged, I thought, with satisfaction. These were the very doubts she had voiced when I had told her I had been given a car. I hope she will remember this one time when I did not express my feelings, though I was dismayed and disgruntled. I did not say it would be a poor return for the generosity of the lenders to put away their car for a week. Certainly this had not been the purpose of the loan. I did not say I thought it unlikely there would be nothing of interest to see beyond the confines of the Seine and the Yonne. And I did not say I considered the Captain's objections a challenge. I am not aware ordinarily of intangibles in the air. I hear people say, "Couldn't you feel the animosity or the coldness or the warmth?" I seem able only to register, like a thermometer, that a room is warm or cold; but that evening I did sense the young Captain was tautened by the responsibilities a new group of passengers imposed, the adjustments involved and the technique of getting a boat under way. Therefore, I told him his suggestion was probably the practical one. On the way back to rejoin the others Sophy asked if I felt all right.

His announcement of dinner gave us the first view of Jacques the chef. Captain Richard, introducing him, explained the name was actually Joachim but Jacques the easier and favored appellation. As a stove gives off heat Jacques gave off vitality and gaiety. They came from his stocky muscular build, crisp black hair, lively dark eyes, pink cheeks, very white teeth, a smile and overall expression of amusement and eagerness to participate in whatever was going on around him. I had no reason to change my first impression. Jacques was not a shy, self-effacing, unnoticeable person. In his daytime moments of leisure he joined whatever persons were on board, sometimes to read a paper, sometimes to vouchsafe information or philosophy. In his evening hours of relaxation he played the harmonica in the saloon when he remained on board. Other evenings with that instrument in his pocket he would set off on his bicycle for a café or any other form of entertainment the nearest village might afford. I never saw a man play with such lusty enjoyment, such involvement of the whole body, from stamping feet to shaking shoulders and nodding head; nor with such blissful unawareness of tune and harmony. It was always a surprise when a few notes in sequence would disclose a familiar air.

Another picture that comes immediately to my mind without turning to my photograph album is of Jacques on his bicycle. He is returning from an early-morning shopping ex-

pedition to the village. Strapped horizontally across a sort of platform behind the saddle, and extending on either side, wide beyond the bicycle itself, is a mountainous pile of bread loaves. They have just come from the oven and will still be warm when we break them at the breakfast table; by the end of the last meal of the day there will not be left a single loaf to break. They will have been stored upright in a receptacle that looks like a laundry hamper, the lid opened and the loaves drawn out when required. On the bicycle in a large basket hooked to the handlebars there are fresh croissants also hot, and vegetables. The load is considerable but Jacques pedals unconcernedly and effortlessly along the towpath, and as he bicycles he reads the morning paper he has just purchased. When he looks up it is not to be watchful of the path he is traveling but in the hope of an audience on the deck of the *Palinurus*. When this hope is realized he grins joyfully, waves enthusiastically with the hand that until that moment has been steering his vehicle (the other is employed to hold his newspaper). Then, waving and reading so that we may see he can do both, he puts on a burst of speed, arriving at the gangplank with a flourish and a shouted, "Bonjour, j'arrive."

As a harmonica player Jacques is not a musician but as a chef he is an artist. Dinner that first night was a gourmet's delight and almost overwhelming. It began with a pea soup of a consistency not too thick, not too thin, but like the little bear's porridge, just right. Our next course was grilled herring, sweet, delicate, golden brown. A roast of veal subtly flavored came next, with *pommes soufflées* and string beans. The salad was plain lettuce, the kind that seems only to occur in France, where the lettuce is both so fresh it seems to have been brought from the garden only an hour before and at the same time "fatigued" to limpness. With this was a tray of assorted cheeses and finally fruit and almonds. Four bottles of the *vin du pays* marched the length of the table and at either end a long basket held the bread. The bread precipitated a downfall happily accepted by every dieter there. Days of atonement would come later.

David sat next to me. I do not remember who sat on my other side. Whoever sat beyond David had small satisfaction from him, because I wanted to talk about canals. I had been on the English waterways twice, I told him.

When he heard that, his shyness melted. He came from a long line of barge people, he said. When I asked if he had grown up on a barge he looked embarrassed and said disgustedly, "They put me ashore for schooling." Grinning through his beard, he added, "But you see I'm back on the water again and I always will be."

When I asked him about the grapevine I'd been told extended the length of every waterway, he corroborated the things I had learned: news of barge people travels along the ways with a rapidity to challenge telegram or telephone, even though the barges themselves move so slowly. David said also barge people were clannish and secretive and I had heard this. They did not mingle with land folk, were even suspicious of them. It was a rare privilege for an outsider to be invited onto a barge, but among themselves they were very hospitable. The women were as house proud as any on the land, kept their brasses and copper polished so you could see yourself in them "and that's not easy when you're hauling coal." They set great store by their utensils; copper or brass, or tin painted all over solid with flowers and fruits. I told him I owned one of these, a scoop for dipping water from the canal to be used for cooking. On a canal trip in England I had bought it from a man who made them. David was impressed.

"They're not easy to come by," he said. "Very few people left who make them."

David told me too the bargewomen were proud of the souvenirs they collected to show the places they had been both in England and other countries, wherever the waterways took them and there were jobs to be hauled.

"Souvenirs to show off," he said, "are about the only things that will take a woman off her boat."

The dinner and the length of a day that had begun at five o'clock hung heavy over our eyes. We said good night soon after we left the table and went to bed. From my cabin I heard a few faint cries for the *pompier,* but if there were other sounds later I was too deep in sleep to hear them.

6

AT breakfast the next morning I heard a sound that brought me to my feet. On every passenger ship I've known, this sound marks the moment of departure.

"Here it is," I said loudly, "the big moment. Shouldn't we do something? There aren't any passengers going ashore but maybe we ought to go out on deck and wave anyway."

Some members of the group were still below and I called down the stairs to them. Those at tables half started to rise but looked bewildered. Cornelia at the far end of the room toward the stern lifted her voice.

"Emily," she said, "what's the matter with you?"

"Can't you hear it?" I asked in some exasperation. "The 'all passengers ashore' signal. We're going to pull away. This is *it*."

"If you mean that banging noise," was her answer, "it's Emma in the scullery, scraping a saucepan; something is probably stuck to the bottom of it."

I sat down again.

"By the way," she added, "we've been under way quite some time."

After all the weeks of anticipation and preparation the moment of actual climax had slid by, flattened out.

There was nothing anticlimactic about the journey itself that day. We were on the Seine and we were looking at the forest of Fontainebleau, punctuated at wide intervals by châteaux, some small, some very large. Each had a garden and these varied in size and elaborateness of design, but were constant in their brightness of color. Neill was gleeful as a little boy, focusing the binoculars he had brought and calling out or pausing to write in a little notebook the names of things blooming. Cornelia vouchsafed a piece of information that startled me. Over the years she has ascribed to me a characteristic she maintains she does not find in other people. I make up explanations, she says, for things I either do not understand or cannot identify. I am not aware of this trait because it does not occur to me there can be an explanation other than the one of my own making. I did recognize, however, a discrepancy when she called attention to the prevalence of mistletoe in the trees along the way. When I said I hadn't seen any she pointed it out to me.

"I thought those were rookeries," I told her. I was asked severally to tell them what a rookery was, and I was happy to oblige. From novels I had read I knew rookeries were places in which rooks nested. Pressed for definition of a rook, I said a rook, obviously, was a bird that lived in a rookery. According to my reading in English novels, these residences were in towers of castles usually haunted, or in bare trees stark against the landscape. The trees holding what I assumed to be nests were more bare than those in the vicinity. Therefore, they had been chosen by rooks. They were bare, Cornelia told me, because mistletoe is a parasite and kills the other foliage. I grew very tired of rookeries being shown to me. I knew then I would not share other explanations I might develop along the trip.

We were sitting on the deck wrapped in coats and other coverings because, though the sun was bright, the air was chilly. We were drowsy with contentment in the slow pace at which we moved, enabling us to savor and share details of the scenes we were passing. Suddenly we were aware of a quickening movement around us. Richard—we had dropped the title of Captain now at his request—ran past us to the bow, gathered up a coil of rope there and stood poised for motion. Sophy and I, sitting up at the same moment, smiled at each other. Because we had traveled on English canals* we knew on the instant what was about to happen. The others came out of their cocoons with rapidity. We lined the rail on either side.

A cascade of short, sharp notes behind us like a small dog barking turned our heads as if we were puppets. In the stern on his high platform bearded David at the wheel, like a Biblical prophet, was blowing into a long tin horn. Our heads turned from him to see what had prompted the trumpeting. In that instant when our attention had shifted, the scene ahead had changed. Leaning far over the rail we could see, beyond the barges that intervened, lock gates slowly opening. David's horn stopped. There were no sounds from the boats around us, but on an instant, as if an audible command had been given, the line ahead of us began to move and we in turn were in quicker motion. We did not know the reason for it but we admitted to one another afterward each had sensed a tension between Richard and David. David eased us to the

* And a Right Good Crew.

right of the boat just ahead and as we reached that place the gates behind us closed. Richard turned around facing us but looking over our heads at David. Raising his hands clasped above his head, he shook them in an unmistakable gesture of triumph. He called out, "We made it."

With the closing of the gates the water rose beneath, lifting all the craft in the channel. It is a curious feeling, like being in a freight elevator, except that in an elevator there is no sensation of being either pulled or pushed up. In a lock there is an acute awareness of a giant strength pushing up.

The doors from the saloon banged open. Margalo stood in the doorway, breathless and wide-eyed. "Is it a waterspout?" she inquired.

The whole company was on deck, I had thought, but she had been quietly playing solitaire, she said.

Babel answered her, everyone delighting in showing off his newborn superiority and exchanging impressions of his sensations in the experience. No one knew the reason for the signaled triumph between Captain and pilot until Richard on his way to the stern at a run called back to us, "We're the last one let in."

We watched him throw a rope around one of the stanchions placed at intervals along the broad top of the stone walls that confine the lock channel. Now we had opportunity to look at the barges drawn alongside. Through their windows we had glimpses of domesticity in the wheelhouses that were both charming and touching. There were lace curtains tied back with ribbons and bows, plants on every sill so closely set we might have been looking into a conservatory. On one, emptied of its load, the lady of the barge had taken advantage of the area made vacant, and hung out her wash on a line that went from bow to stern in the hollow of the boat. Looking down on it we saw this household included lace and embroidered antimacassars and pink sheets. I repeated the facts

of barge life David had told me at dinner.

As I talked the gates opened and we moved slowly ahead and out of the lock. Immediately beyond it a string of barges was moored to the bank on our port side. (We were beginning to toss nautical terms into our conversation.) Each barge was decorated with gay pennants strung from bow to stern and across. Neither Sophy nor I could give an explanation for this. Romney thought it must be a regatta of some sort.

Jacques interrupted. We had not heard him come on deck, but we were not surprised that he broke into our conversation.

"No, no, no," he said in French, "a wedding. Two barge people are getting married. On the other barges with flags are relatives, maybe some friends. There will be gala two, three days."

Jacques had come to tell us lunch was served. Leading the way to the table, he tossed back another bit of information: we had now left the Seine and were on the River Loing. We sat down to a gourmet's dream so attractively presented Brother took photographs of the trays of food as they were set on the table. That day as I remember we began with *potage,* the rest of the meal was of cold dishes, and this was always true, but sometimes we began with shrimps in the shell or artichokes vinaigrette. After that, trays of cold meats, another of radishes, lettuce, cucumbers, raw carrots, and always for dessert cheese and fruit—apples, oranges, pears.

Understandably, after lunch, there was a slacking off in activity, even conversation. Albert was asleep in the saloon, comfortably settled into a low armchair, when we entered the next lock. Romney was playing solitaire; Margalo, Frances and I were on the deck. An army veteran, wearing his medals, came alongside in a motor wheelchair. He called up to us, asking if we would like to buy the toys he made, by hand, he emphasized. They were charming tiny horses of leather, gaily painted. We called back we would, and asked him to wait while we got our money. When we came up the stairs from our cabins Frances was speaking urgently to Albert. She interrupted herself to say impatiently over her shoulder, "Of course, I want to contribute, but Albert has all the money."

Returning her attention to him she shook him gently and spoke. I would have considered it an unusual summons from sleep on a barge, but Albert responded.

"Wake up, darling," Frances said, "please wake up and buy me a little horse."

"Of course," was Albert's response. "What day of the week is it?"

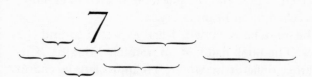

7

AT about four o'clock in the afternoon we eased gently over to the right (starboard) bank and moored there. We had reached the first port on our voyage, Moret-sur-Loing. Richard tossed heavy spikes, a hatchet and then himself to the bank; he drove the spikes into the ground at intervals. David, leaving the wheel, came to the deck and dropped ropes that Richard attached. David then swung out a diminutive gangplank, painted white; Richard secured that also to the ground. A handrail followed that was fitted into slots along one side the gangplank, and the way was ready for passengers to disembark. They were ready too.

Ahead in the distance we could see the spire of a church, and made this our direction finder. Walking along the towpath we were in small groups of two or three close to one another, but reaching the town itself we scattered suddenly and widely. I do not know why we did this, no one mentioned to the others a particular objective, but on that instant a pattern was set for every stopping place. Later we talked a little about it only because Neill had the most remarkable talent for disappearing any of us had ever seen. Entering the town he was always with someone; the next instant he was nowhere. It did not seem possible, we said, for a man so tall and proportionately solid to melt away. Neill melted. He always knew from his assiduous pursuit of guidebooks exactly what he expected to find and the places he wished to explore, but how he reached them I cannot say.

Reading the guidebook myself, I had expected to find the streets narrow. The book had said, to translate literally, "Circulation is rather difficult in Moret. To appreciate its charm one should leave one's car in one of the parking lots and walk on foot in the city."

The streets are indeed narrow, and charming. Where there are sidewalks, these are very narrow too. I walked along them and then like other pedestrians moved into the street. There were very few cars. I paused now and then to look into shop windows, of course, and certainly in the windows of antique shops. I even entered one. The only time during my exploration of Moret that I displayed haste was in the speed with which I backed out of that antique shop, learning that the price of an unremarkable but pleasant Quimper plate I had seen in the window was $65.

Not far ahead, perhaps a block, I recognized Albert. Frances was with him. They had stopped before a window. My attention was directed to them because Albert was facing the street, looking up and down and waving a beckoning gesture in every direction. This semaphore action brought Brother and Emily from a side lane. I came up eagerly. Knowing Frances's love of antiques I was sure she had spotted

some gems, though I was not sure I would go in to price them. It was not Frances's discovery that had charged Albert into action; it was his own: Edison, Marconi and Dr. Salk could not have been more triumphant.

"Look," he said as we converged. "French ice cream. Real French ice cream and vanilla, too."

The Hacketts were in front of a patisserie. Frances explained there was nothing in the world so delicious to Albert as French ice cream. "He's on its trail all over Paris, even New York."

Emily responded immediately. Albert was not aware of my apologetic refusal; he was bustling Emily inside. Frances chose to wait for them. Brother and I walked on. At the moment we caught sight of Margalo and Cornelia we saw the church and stood gaping at the façade and beautiful portals in what the guidebook calls "flamboyant Gothic style."

Brother said he did not want to go in without Emily since this would be the first church she would see in France. Turning we saw her coming, a beatific look on her face as she licked an ice-cream cone. She responded to our beckoning by hurrying to join us. When she saw the façade and realized it was not another patisserie to which she had been summoned, she faced an awful decision. She would not ask us to wait until she had finished the last crumb of the cone, nor hurry its savoring, nor throw it away, nor enter a church licking at it. She compromised. With one hand she pulled a scarf from around her neck, placed it on her head, and entered the church, the ice-cream cone behind her. We thought she had sacrificed it, but, leaving the church with a last look back, we were mortified by the sight of a trail of blobs of melted ice cream that betrayed our passage; Emily was disgruntled only because all the ice cream had gone into the trail, the tip of the empty cone remained. She would have thought, she said, the temperature and the sanctity of this interior would have preserved it.

The church of Notre Dame was begun in the middle of the twelfth century, and consecrated by Thomas Becket, the Archbishop of Canterbury, the guidebook had told us. *We* discovered that its windows are beautiful; the statue of the mother and child on the left near the entrance is stark and deeply moving.

Outside, we separated again without explanation, but a few minutes later on a street not far from the church I came again upon Brother and Emily and joined them. We kept to the sidewalk, but we walked single file, Emily ahead. Brother discovered and stopped in front of a camera shop. He was running out of flash bulbs, he told me over his shoulder, and asked if I would go in with him to help with the language. With a modesty he knew was affected, I said I would try. If I am stopped in the pursuit of the French language I flounder, therefore I do not permit interruption.

As the shopkeeper came toward us I began. We were searching for lights for our camera, I told him, that would permit one to photograph interiors. I may have told him, too, a little about our barge trip. My daughters say it is impossible for me to make the simplest request without including a considerable portion of my life history and theirs. What I did say to the shopkeeper occupied some little time and perhaps considerable wordage. When I had finished with what I considered a rather fine flourish the clerk inquired:

"A flash bulb?"

Such moments are discomfiting to an earnest traveler who wants to establish rapport in a foreign field.

Emerging from the shop, Brother made a very poor effort to conceal his relish of the incident, but my annoyance was only a slight ripple compared to the indignation evidenced in the very way she walked as Emily came toward us.

"You Kimbroughs," she told us, *"you* Vanishing Kimbroughs. I've never felt such a fool."

She had walked on, she told us, unaware that we were no longer behind her. She had addressed a considerable conversation to us and only after some time, aware of no response from behind, had turned around to discover the pavement empty of Kimbroughs and everyone else. The only person in the vicinity was a painter on a ladder above the spot where she had stopped.

"He was looking down with interest," she said bitterly, "on a solitary woman walking the pavement, talking in a loud voice at space."

We apologized, but Brother, with deft perceptiveness of how she could best be restored to her usual happy nature, bought her another ice-cream cone.

Unexpectedly we were back at the church again, but though Emily had finished her cone we did not visit it a second time. We had seen to the right of its façade a beautiful half-timbered building and knew from the guidebook this was the *hospice* built in the fifteenth century, where nuns still make and sell a barley-sugar candy for which the place is famous.

A sign on the door told us we were within the hours when it was open, but the door itself seemed to be locked. We were turning away when we were hailed by a passerby, a woman carrying on one arm a large full market basket and with the other hand leading a little girl perhaps four years old. Setting down the market basket she came with the child to the threshold where we were standing.

Indicating a bell we had not seen, she said, "Il faut sonner, vous voyez."

She had walked a distance from the place she had deposited her market basket and we thanked her for taking the trouble.

She assured us it had been no trouble at all; it would have been a pity for us to turn away from this place because the candy was delicious and the nuns were so nice. She hoped we were having a pleasant time. Were we English? When we told her we were Americans she said to the little girl, "You must shake hands with these Americans, and wish them a happy visit to France." As I took the child's hand, smiling over her head at the mother, a good part was erased in my mind of the hateful sign on the wall outside Fontaine-bleau.

The sister who waited on us was warm and friendly, stout, ruddy-cheeked, with smiling eyes and mouth. She pressed upon us as a gift a little bag of the sort of candy we had not purchased.

Along the winding street on which the hospice stands Neill materialized.

"A little farther on," he told us, "you'll find the house where Sisley lived for twenty years. He painted everything around here. You can't go in but there's a plaque on the gate and you can see the skylight of his studio above the trees. Across from it is the old dungeon but it's now a school or at least a place where small children can be boarded. That's what the sign outside says."

He was gone, dematerialized I suppose. We saw Sisley's house and the one-time dungeon, a timbered structure ("*pans de bois*"), like the hospice. Fouquet—I like to believe he was the man in the Iron Mask—was imprisoned there during his four-year trial. This was the first cross-timbered architecture I had seen in France. I had identified the style with England, but we were to see it repeated in other places we visited.

Back on "la Grande Rue," the guidebook identifies it, we realized we had made a full circuit. A high tower at each end of the *rue* marks the boundaries of the town. The towers are what remain of the fourteenth-century encircling fortifications. Each tower is supported by a beautiful archway. We walked under the one Brother said would bring us back to the river. I never question anyone's statement about anything geographic. I would have gone in the opposite direction, but he was right.

The long and beautiful bridge over the river was demolished during the war, the guidebook says, but has been completely reconstructed to its original design. Neill was on the bridge.

"Margalo and Cornelia are down there having tea," he said, pointing to a place below, along the riverbank. "It's a charming little café."

He must have looked down on them as he floated by overhead. When we asked if he had seen any of the others he pointed again in the direction from which we had come.

"Do you see that little shop just at the end of the bridge? You passed it. Frances and Albert are inside. Do you know what it sells?"

"Postcards," we answered simultaneously, and he nodded. We had only been in Fontainebleau and Samois and in those places a very short time, but we had already learned Frances and Albert buy postcards, but not as other travelers buy them, sporadically and sparsely. The Hacketts buy them *en gros,* some for sending, some for keeping.

"I haven't kept postcards since I was ten," Cornelia had whispered to me when we shared our discovery about the Hacketts. "Mother made me. In an album."

As the gangplank was being assembled at Moret, even before it was put down, I had heard Frances say, "Albert, the first thing we must do is to find the post office and send some of our cards."

Immediately on the word "postcards," as if they had heard the cue, Frances and Albert came from the shop. Seeing us,

Frances called out as they approached, "You really must get some cards there; the prettiest we've seen."

When they had reached us, Albert said delightedly, "The most extraordinary thing. Several years ago we motored through here. The man in that shop remembered us."

I was not surprised. I doubt the man had made, from that time until a few minutes ago, so large a sale.

Sam and Sophy joined us, coming from the opposite side of the bridge. They were worn out, Sophy assured us. They had walked miles.

"Around the town?" Emily asked. "We didn't see you."

Sophy looked indignantly at each of us in turn. "You mean you didn't know Sam and I got off at the last lock and walked from there?"

Frances is chronically distressed by a possibility of having hurt someone's feelings.

"Darling," she asked urgently, "Do forgive us. I'm afraid we didn't notice. We were buying little horses."

"We saw the town before you arrived," Sam told us, "but after that we couldn't find the *boat* again."

Sophy interposed. She does not like her geographic stability to be accused of wavering.

"I've never known anyone in my life," she said, "even Emily, with such a complete absence of sense of direction as Sam. He thought we'd been traveling from exactly the opposite way, and wanted to go *back* along the part of the river we haven't even *reached* yet."

Sam admitted this happily, "I doubt there's anyone gets lost as often and as easily."

Sophy continued. "I persuaded him we had to go the opposite way and sure enough we found the *Palinurus*, but we were on the other side of the river from it. We could see Romney sitting in the saloon."

"Playing solitaire no doubt," Neill interjected.

Sophy nodded. "We called to him. He came out on deck. Told us all of you had gone into Moret. He had explored a little too but doesn't like churches, he said, so he'd come back."

"Then we came all the way here again," Sam took up the recital, "and finally we found you. No thanks to me."

We lingered on the bridge, going from one side to the other with deep enjoyment of the view each way. On our right were a few houses. The one nearest the gate was particularly charming, set unevenly along and on top of a steep cliff high above the river. The entrance from the bridge was through a small gate, then across a narrow footbridge over a tiny branch of the river.

Behind it the church made a backdrop. On the other side of the bridge and directly below we looked down on a vine-covered stone building filling a tiny spit of land. Brother was the first to catch sight of the millstone half buried in vines that identified the building. Two weeks later, in Paris, Emily, Brother, Sophy and I went to the Orangerie to see an exhibition of the French Impressionists on loan from Swiss collections. In a room given over to Sisleys, though we did not know this when we stood in the doorway, Brother pointed across to the opposite wall.

"That without any question," he said, "is the old mill below the bridge at Moret."

We did not question and we found immediately with joy other Sisleys that carried us back nostalgically to that late afternoon in Moret.

The General made a suggestion as we stood on the bridge. The spot on which she stood when making it should have a marker.

"Why don't I hire a taxi here, go back to Samois, pick up our car and bring it alongside the *Palinurus?*"

There had been no mention of the Volkswagen dilemma

since our conversation with Richard the evening before, but it had been on my mind all day and I had not been happy with it.

We applauded; we told her only a general could have evolved such a brilliant maneuver. Her chagrin that her absence had not been noticed was erased by her pleasure in our applause. Neill and Sam asked eagerly to go with her. Less than an hour later, only a few minutes after the rest of us had returned, our dear Volkswagen drew up alongside the *Palinurus* and we cheered. Sophy came to my cabin while I was dressing for dinner.

"I thought you might like to know," she said, "it took us just under fifteen minutes to reach the car" (it had been a six-hour trip by barge), "and cost five dollars. Divided among eleven people I think this is not excessive, and the drive was heavenly." Fifteen minutes was the longest span of time needed to retrieve the car during the remainder of our trip, and that day the only one in which we did not explore, in the car, surrounding countryside, encompassing a far wider area than would have been possible afoot or on bicycle.

At dinner we reviewed characteristics the day's expedition had revealed: Albert's love of French ice cream; the Hacketts' passion for postcards, though this had not been totally unexpected; Neill's extraordinary gift for invisibility.

"Like the Vanishing Kimbroughs," Emily interjected. Romney insisted the most remarkable of all was the revelation of Sam's lack of sense of direction and asked if it had not complicated his work. At Sam's look of bewilderment he explained.

"If I were going to have an operation I'd certainly want you to do it, but I'd be glad to know there was an assistant standing by to say, 'Oops, doctor! Wrong turn. The appendix is over this way.' "

8

COMING upstairs or on top, whatever the Admiral would call it, next morning for breakfast I went on deck first to smell the day. The smell was deeply satisfying and so was the sight. A blue sky, bright sun, not so much breeze as the day before, a warmer air with the scent of lilacs in it. Someone calling good morning startled me but not so much as the discovery it was Margalo and that she had already breakfasted and, wrapped in a coat, was settled in a deck chair reading. Her head was protected from the sun by an idiotic little tricorne bonnet of linen tied under the chin, but that was not what had surprised me. Margalo always dresses with style, individuality—and humor. What had astonished me was that she should be there at all and I told her so.

"Oh," she said, "I'm not the only one up and about. Sophy

and Sam and Albert have gone for a walk."

There was no news value in that bit of information, I assured her.

"If you'd told me Sophy was having breakfast in bed and Sam was playing solitaire I would have counted that worth remarking on. You're the bit of news. Everyone I know in the theatre doesn't meet the day until at least eleven."

"I always get up early" was Margalo's answer. "You can add that to the list of characteristics we're discovering."

Neill, coming through the door to the deck, overheard this. "I'll give you another," he said. "I took it for granted with her wonderful ear for accent and, well, general sophistication, of course she would speak French fluently, but you don't, do you?"

Margalo shuddered. I answered for her. "She's allergic to the language. Even hearing it can make her come out in spots."

By a tacit understanding, or a form of ESP, Neill and I went to separate tables for breakfast. My reason for moving to a table of my own was an inner conviction I was going to eat both a croissant and French bread with marmalade on it and I did not wish anyone to witness my gluttony.

Through an open window by my table I saw Richard leave the boat, a suitcase in each hand. He had evidently taken ashore previously a bicycle. I watched him strap the two suitcases behind its saddle. My immediate interpretation was that the Captain was deserting his ship but simultaneously wondered if this could be the kind of explanation to myself Cornelia had derided. Richard's fiancée, Jean, passed my window in the narrow corridor outside. She was scarcely recognizable in smart city clothes. Perhaps they were eloping, but Richard did not look dressed for it. Even to me that explanation, too, seemed unlikely. I called out to tell her I was sorry she was leaving.

She hated to go, she said, "But the holidays are over, I have to get back to my job. Richard's riding me to the station."

There was the *dea ex machina!* Except she was not going to be out of a machine; she was going to be in one, mine, and I would bless her.

"Richard," I said, and I hoped my voice had the quality of a cooing dove, *"please* take the Volkswagen. There it is."

There had been no mention to him of its arrival the night before, nor that it was parked a few feet away from the *Palinurus.*

"You'll be dead riding Jean and those suitcases all the way to the station and you'll ruin her clothes."

Richard looked up all smiles.

"That's awfully good of you," he said, "if you're sure you don't mind. I have my driver's license with me."

I waved graciously toward the car. "Take it," I said, "the keys are in the glove compartment."

He was unstrapping the suitcases as I talked. Jean thanked me fervently.

"I really wasn't looking forward to riding all that way on the handlebars."

Richard put the suitcases in the car, reached in, extracted the keys, saw Jean into the seat beside the driver's, closed the door, and came back to the edge of the bank.

"I was just thinking," he said, "perhaps it would be a good idea for me to put the bicycle in the car, leave the car at the station, where it would be completely safe, perhaps safer than here. I'll bring the keys to you and tomorrow you can hire a taxi in Sens to bring you back to pick up your car, no distance at all."

"What a splendid idea," I told him, and waited until they were out of sight to execute a little pas seul of triumph.

From that time on it was Richard who suggested places to

visit in the car and timed his schedule to accommodate its overnight parking spot.

Shortly after the departure of the sad young lovers Jennifer came through the saloon and I stopped her to ask about them. She told me they had met at the University of Reading, where they were both students. They loved each other. They were engaged. They wanted to marry, but Jean had continued at the University of Reading, taken her degree and gone on to a master's. She had a very good job teaching retarded children. Richard had left the university to follow the waterways. They were rivers apart in the way they wanted to live, Jean in a house ashore and Richard forever on the water. How this would be bridged Jennifer did not know, but perhaps time and the seasons themselves would do it. Waterways were not navigable through the winter and schools were not in session all summer. There was hope.

The day was sunny, with a breeze to make coats welcome on the deck, and that was where we wanted to be. We had been on the Loing in order to visit Moret. Then we had retraced our route and were on the Seine again. The landscape was a delight. Apple trees were in bloom; green meadows were slashed by bands of yellow mustard, more intense than a patch of sunlight and reaching as far as the eye could stretch. The route took us into a succession of locks, our passage through each one a separate and absorbing experience. We began to recognize the dexterity of our pilot. We were talking about this when Jennifer, going along the outer corridor toward the stern, heard us and stopped.

"You ought to hear some of our passengers talking to David," she said and laughed. "He says he can always spot a landlubber who doesn't know a thing about boats or navigation. The fellow always says bringing a boat into a lock must be so simple anybody could do it. 'It's right there in front of you,' he says, 'nowhere else to go. All you have to do is head for it and slip right in.'

"If they only knew how tricky it is," she explained, "to run a long boat from the stern! You have to gauge what to allow for a cross breeze that may come up, shift your speed on the instant, and your timing has to be of the split second." She pointed to an upright slender pole in the center of the bow.

"When we get into the Burgundy Canal," she told us, "the Captain will tell you never to stand in the way of that pole. It's David's indicator. The canal is so narrow and the bridges so low if he doesn't hold the boat to dead center he'll crack us either against the side or into the bridge. Have you seen a black cat?"

The change of subject only seemed startling, I explained to myself. It was probably the thing to say so that the accidents she was talking about would not actually happen; like two people saying "bread and butter" to each other to avoid a quarrel when they have let something come between them.

"It's a cat that came aboard at Samois," Jennifer was saying. "Poor little thing, it was chased by a big tom. We got him off but she's still on board somewhere and she's going to have kittens. The tom didn't get to her, but she's so scared she's hiding somewhere. I put food out and I keep calling her. I'm so afraid she'll hide in a spot we can't reach. David's helping me look every chance he gets. If you do see her please call me as fast as you can but don't make any move toward her or you'll scare her away again. I've named her Miranda."

I was distressed about the cat, but glad I had not vouchsafed my explanation of Jennifer's query.

Traffic held us up outside one lock for a little over two hours with not a moment of boredom in them. There was a constant flow of barges coming up behind and alongside. In the canal we would move single file, but here on the broad

Seine it was not unlike Fifth Avenue at rush hour, every taxi driver jockeying for a place ahead of his neighbors. A barge that was our nearest neighbor during the wait displayed on its bow a life-size and realistic statue of a Dalmatian dog in painted clay, spots and all, probably a monument to a dear departed.

The traffic of our own group moved. Some went below for a nap, some read. Margalo and Romney played solitaire at separate tables, Neill read maps and guidebooks, Frances wrote postcards, Cornelia worked on a piece of tapestry. I reluctantly looked for and found Richard. I had been prodded by my companions to make an unlikely complaint about our dinners. There was too much content; we were surfeited. Cornelia and Sophy had conveyed to me the delicacy of this mission and their doubt I could accomplish it successfully, pointing out delicacy was not my usual avenue of approach. With equal emphasis they refused to take it on, explaining that if Jacques considered this a slight to his artistry he would undoubtedly quit the job and neither of them wished to assume responsibility for this. I seldom buckle under pressure, but I yielded because I might accomplish a mission of my own at the same time.

Frances and Albert were involved in mine. We are victims of a reaction to onion, garlic or any of their relatives so violent as to make us distressingly ill even when we have not detected a telltale flavor or aroma. To ask a French chef not to use these ingredients I knew would be like asking Mr. Rubinstein to play the piano with only one hand. I made what I consider an adroit detour around the first request. I made it by way of the Captain. No instinct for etiquette nor protocol directed me; it was cowardice. I did not reveal this to Richard when he expressed his appreciation of my knowledge of correct procedure.

"There are passengers," he said, "who do not seem to know that whatever concerns the crew should be dealt with by the Captain."

Smiling with, I hope, becoming modesty at my superior knowledge, I told him our complaint; we were being given too much to eat. Our dinner last night had begun with a beautiful cream soup; our next course had been two kinds of fish, plaice and whitebait; a roast of lamb had followed with mushrooms and string beans; and the finale a dessert of sour cream, cream cheese and sugar like a *coeur à la crème* (Emily is determined to try it at home, and with her figure, she can).

My suggestion was that Richard put reduction on the basis of economy not of our figures.

"Then Jacques cannot think we are not enjoying his food."

Richard was surprised by the complaint, but pleased by my suggested approach.

"You won't be brought into it at all," he assured me. "I'll tell him I noticed none of our passengers this trip eat as much as we generally provide. If we provide less, they will be satisfied, and we can save on food. No Frenchman can resist logic or thrift. I'll give him both."

That was the moment for me to move on to onions; success was in my hands. I think the reason I held back was a hesitancy to criticize quantity and quality at the same time. As the detective stories say, how bitterly I was to regret this!

The General was pleased with my report, so were the others hearing it; they had moved again to the deck. I went back to the saloon and the little table I had appropriated. I wanted to bring my notes to date. I was startled by Jacques's voice, and looked up.

"Regardez, regardez," he was calling, pointing out a window as he came from the kitchen almost at a run. I looked in the direction he indicated but saw nothing spectacular nor alarming in the landscape.

"It is necessary that you write this down." He stood by my table and indicated my notebook. "It is very important. Look, as I tell you." I do not know why he had moved into English.

"We are passing," he said, "at this very moment," his voice trembling a little between excitement and reverence, "the archaeological center of France. I will tell you. Twenty-five thousand years ago the hommes come down from the mountains on that side to hunt the bestials, and so the bestials come down from the mountain on the other side to this river for the water. And so the hommes kill the bestials and eat them and now the pipples have found the skeens and the bones of the bestials, and the pipples of twenty-five thousand years ago. So they are steel digging but only in le saison because it is too cold and the ground is too solide in the winter. And so I have a dog, an Alsatian, but I cannot certainly keep him on this barge. I could have him then only in the winter, so I have geeven him to the archaeological because he protects all those bones and skeens. And so you see it is the greatest center in France."

Indeed the caves of Arcy are famous. In the guidebook, description of their wonders does not mention Jacques's dog.

As I thanked him for his remarkable information I would not have found in a guidebook, it occurred to me this was a propitious moment to speak about onions. Jacques was beaming with pride of knowledge, and satisfaction with my enthusiastic gratitude. With this *entente cordiale* between us, I could waive correct procedures.

He listened, nodding gravely, as I explained our digestive unhappiness and begged him to sacrifice his artistry to our eccentricity.

"You may have all confidence in me, madame." He had reverted to French. "You, Mme. and M. Hackett will not have even a small malaise. It is I who assures you."

We shook hands for some reason, while I thanked him. He returned to his atelier.

Even the insatiable walkers did not leave the boat that day after the pre-breakfast stretch, even for sprints along the towpaths. They fretted a little but conceded the necessity for the Captain's request not to quit the boat. Timing at the locks is uncertain and yet must be exact, he had explained. Even if his boat is well up in the line of those waiting to enter a lock the Captain cannot be certain his will be included in the first lot. Here the lock keeper's authority is absolute. When the moments of entry and exit do arrive they must be realized on the instant or the boat dawdling will lose its hard-won place in line. Certainly there is not time to gather in passengers strolling along the path.

In spite of these precautions and our advantageous position in line, the *Palinurus* was rejected at one of the locks, forcing another delay of two hours. We did not moor for the night until nearly six o'clock, on the outskirts of a little town Richard told us was called Courlon-sur-Yonne. We could see we were opposite a row of neat houses, each with a garden in front, and in the center of the row a café. At our approach, the proprietor came out, a white apron tied about his middle. Two fat dogs followed him to the bank and tussled halfheartedly while he vigorously waved a towel in the air to welcome our approach. As we came within hearing distance we realized he was also calling an invitation to visit his establishment. From their enthusiastic greeting I realized he and Richard were firm friends and that the *Palinurus* had come to rest there before. Emma, Jacques and Jennifer came on deck to wave and call greetings and David blew a salute on his horn.

We visited the establishment after dinner. The interior was plain, scrubbed and hospitable. Tables and chairs occupied three-quarters of the room; there were amusing prints on the wall. A bar faced the door and was administered by the wife and daughter of the proprietor, the daughter dark-haired, pretty and shy, the wife ample and beaming like her husband. He hustled among the tables pulling out chairs, rearranging the groupings according to his ideas of our greater enjoyment. The two dogs we had seen with him on the bank followed him, making our progress through the room a little difficult. One of the dogs had the markings of a springer spaniel. The proprietor hearing me identify the other as a Doberman corrected.

"Not at all, madame," he assured me. "She is the daughter of that one," indicating the springer. I have never seen a fainter family resemblance.

The drinks we had ordered were being served when Emma, Jacques and Richard came in and, shortly after, three or four people from the neighborhood. Richard and Emma stood at the bar, Jacques seated himself just inside the door and brought out from a vest pocket his harmonica. We were all gathered into the warmth and friendliness of the room. Its owners and neighbors made us feel we were their welcome guests. Margalo across the table from me leaned forward to murmur, "This is rubbing out that ugly sign on the wall at Fontainebleau."

When the arrival of a glass of wine diverted Jacques from his harmonica, I had an inspiration. I called to the next table, "Bobs, sing! Sing 'La Seine.' "

Cornelia, who maintains, sometimes rightly, she is the most docile of women, obeyed like a soldier at a call to arms, except that her eyes danced and she laughed as she said, "You bet I will."

Her voice is low and true, her French as nearly flawless as

makes no matter, and the song, "La Seine," is loved in every part of France. From the French people at the bar there was first a surprised, delighted recognition, then audible murmurs one to another of the beauty, the perfection of madame's French.

With shoulders shrugging in emphasis, Jacques picked up his harmonica again and, mercifully knowing this song, accompanied her.

When she had come to the end she called out in French, "Come and join me, everybody."

Shyly at first, the French began with her on the second round, gathering volume in their love of the song and their joy in singing it. They drew us all in, even those who did not know the words, because the tune itself is a simple one. We sang it again and again, and other songs, French and American, teaching the French a few words of ours, and even Margalo tried a few words of theirs.

Leaving at last, as I passed Emma and Richard, who was talking to the proprietor, I asked Emma why Jenny and David hadn't come.

"We persuaded Richard to leave the boat for once," Emma said, "but someone had to stay on board. Jenny was longing to join us but David wouldn't let her. He doesn't allow her out of his sight." We shook hands all around.

We came out into a cold, clear, starry night, talking among ourselves as we walked along the bank toward the *Palinurus*. Jennifer's voice from its deck silenced us.

"Listen," she called so urgently we stopped at once. She lowered her voice. "Oh, please listen," she urged softly, "don't you hear? It's a nightingale."

A nightingale sang us on board and to bed that night.

ON my way to breakfast two mornings later I stepped out on deck to feel the air. I needed it. Events of the night before had left me weak-kneed and spent. I had passed the hours spending all my inner resources. Dinner had been a master-piece. An hour later I knew it had included onions. How-ever, what I had lost on the swings I gained on the round-abouts; I learned about Emma. I had found her pretty, gay, intelligent, with charming manners and beautiful French; I had heard her talking to Jacques. I had wondered about her background; it had obviously included education. By way of onions I learned about her kindness, her competence and her life.

She had been reading in the saloon after the others had gone to bed, and heard me when I moaned a little as I sat on the stairs gathering strength to return to my cabin after an upheaval in the bathroom. She had stayed with me until I slept sometime in the early morning, and between my sorties, told me about herself—only because I asked her.

Her mother, a magistrate whose special concern and work is with juveniles, has deep understanding of young people. Therefore, she had sympathy with Emma's longing for self-expression—"You know, trying my hand at lots of things." Emma, speaking of her, made unmistakable their mutual love and respect. Her father "in the city" had been indulgent to her mother's ideas.

Emma's early education had been at a French school in London from the ages of three to thirteen, then at a conventional English school. She had hoped after that to enter St. Martin's School of Art, but she was a year too young. Her mother, because she was a governor of the school, would not use influence nor persuasion. Therefore, Emma went instead to a cooking school, and found this was her métier. She progressed to a cordon bleu course. Since then she had worked in restaurants, and, in order to learn everything a restaurateur needed to know, had been a barmaid. Deciding languages must be included in this knowledge, she had gone to the University of Perugia.

Returning to London, she opened with a friend a restaurant in Chelsea. Working day and night there, she became so run down she had to give it up, but is still a part owner. She saw Richard's advertisement in the *Times* and decided to give it a try. She has loved it, but will not sign on again because she intends to go back to the University of Perugia. Eventually she hopes to get a job in the Common Market—a food buyer for international firms.

When I dropped off to sleep I was giddy and weak, from my ordeal and from the kaleidoscopic image of Emma in bars, restaurants, and university.

The morning air was reviving.

Jacques with bread and vegetables for the day came aboard. He called "Bonjour" as he passed me, but on a sudden thought stopped.

"Madame," he said, "I must tell you something. After you speak to me about the onions I think and think, and then I know what I must do. I make a dish for you last night that gave you great pleasure. I watched you. And, madame, I had placed onions in it, but so subtle you did not know. So you see, madame, all there is that is necessary is to be a good cook who knows how to place the onions."

(Later that day I followed correct procedure: I spoke to the Captain. From that time on the Hacketts and I were served separately an entrée that for the others contained onions. Frances and Albert had not eaten the subtle dish. Frances had been suspicious.)

Richard came on deck. On his way to the bow to cast off he called "Good morning" to me, but paused beside Jacques. Jacques reached around his armload of provisions and they shook hands, saying, "Bonjour, Jacques." "Bonjour, Monsieur le Capitaine."

With a perfection of timing Cornelia looked out the door that instant, saw the encounter, caught my eye and we both laughed in joyful reminiscence and understanding. One of the happiest aspects about a friendship as long as ours is a communication like a secret language established by shared experiences. We both knew at that moment we were back in the room we had shared in a pension in Paris when we were students there. We had been entertained by the French ritual of handshaking on every occasion. We had even seen taxi drivers at a standstill in a traffic block seize the opportunity to reach out from the windows of the respective vehicles and, not without difficulty, exchange a handshake and a "Bonjour." We had conjured up an image of a conjugal morning scene in which husband and wife waking would sit up simultaneously, face each other, extend a hand and say simultaneously, "Bonjour, madame," "Bonjour, monsieur." We had thereupon with glee instituted our own morning rite. At the moment the *femme de chambre* knocked on our door announcing the arrival of our breakfast, we would sit up, each extending a hand around the table between our beds and shaking hands would say with solemnity, "Bonjour, Mademoiselle Kimbrough," "Bonjour, Mademoiselle Skinner."

"Now we know how French Richard has become," I said as I followed her inside for breakfast.

We had been on deck for the departure from Courlon-sur-Yonne. The early hikers, Sophy, Albert and Sam, were telling us with exasperating superiority how much we missed by our sluggishness when Richard executed a feat we had not seen before and was to us an astonishing way of embarking. I was particularly happy the hikers were there to see it at the peak of their superiority. It gave them an idea for emulation that in the execution provided rich entertainment to the rest of us.

With David on deck pulling, Richard from the bank shoved the gangplank on board, leaving himself, we thought, stranded, with far too great a distance for jumping on the boat. He did not jump. David, after stowing the gangplank, drew down from a shallow niche, evidently designed to hold it, a long pole, a boom we had not noticed before because it was so exactly contained. The pole was painted red—to show how hazardous its operation, was my own explanation for the choice of color. The base, on a kind of hinge firmly embedded at the bottom of the niche, allowed the pole to be swung in any direction. David pulled it down to the level of the deck rail and it reached across the water like a gantry crane. As the crane reached him Richard jumped up and like a trapeze artist caught it near its end with both hands.

He pushed off with a vigorous kick from the bank and, dangling over the water, had enough momentum to ride the crane over the water until David, reaching out, pulled it the remaining few feet. Richard, releasing his hold, dropped to the deck. The boom was then tilted up and pushed back into its niche.

The proprietor came out of the café, his wife and daughter following, the mother and daughter dogs frolicking around them. The family waved us off, calling invitations to return. David blew his horn. We all called out good-byes and the *Palinurus* was on her way. Within a few minutes we had rounded a bend in the river and we watched come into view on the opposite shore an avenue of young poplars. The trunks were so bent, probably reaching for sunlight from the heavy undergrowth on either side, the trees formed an arch like a long nave of a cathedral.

Conversation had been sparse, almost monosyllabic. Emily spoke suddenly and decisively. "I know why the Impressionists painted a misty, little bit hazy atmosphere, almost as if they were looking at a landscape through gauze. They painted it that way because that's the way it is. It's a still landscape," she added, "and our boat makes no sound. I feel as if we ought to whisper."

This was something all of us were aware of. I think that is why we talked so little.

I did have something I wanted to tell Frances, but turning to her I forgot what it was in my surprise at seeing her engrossed in the study of a compass held on the extended open palm of her hand. A compass was a piece of equipment I had not thought to bring on this trip. The possibility of losing our way on a river or canal had not occurred to me. I asked if she usually had a compass with her.

"Always," she said, "ever since the first summer Albert and I rented a flat in London, and that was some years ago."

This was another environment in which I would not have thought a compass essential. She explained politely but a little as if she were stating the obvious to a somewhat backward child.

"You must know," she said, "how few sunny days there are in London. Well, of course, we wanted a flat that would get the most whenever there was any. So I bought a compass to take along when we were flat hunting. Then I could see which way the windows faced. I carry it now wherever we go."

Albert sitting beside her joined the conversation.

"It made a fool out of me," he said with a malevolent glance at the little instrument. "We were flying to England last year and Frances had that miserable thing out as usual. I wasn't paying any attention, in fact I was dozing a little, until she shook my arm and told me we were flying in the wrong direction. I told her the pilot probably knew the way from New York to London. I said it was a cheap little compass anyway and probably couldn't register above the ground. I told her she was probably holding it the wrong way round or maybe the instruments on the plane were so strong they pulled that little cheap thing out of line or perhaps the magnetic poles themselves were out of line up in the air and you had to take that into account. I thought they were all good explanations, or at least distracting, but I couldn't shake her. She just kept looking at the thing and repeating we were going in the wrong direction. She was getting more nervous by the minute so I sent for the stewardess. I thought a drink was indicated, but before I could give the order, Frances was in there ahead of me.

"She said, 'We wanted to ask you why we've turned back.'

"The stewardess had the answer. 'Just a little engine trouble,' she said. 'Nothing to worry about.' "

Frances was smiling. "You see," she said, "a compass is a very good thing to have with you."

When I asked, knowing the absurdity of the question, if she was looking at the compass now because of any anxiety, she reassured me seriously.

"Oh, no, but when we rounded that lovely bend, I wanted to see what direction we're following now."

Richard came along the outer gangway and stopped to speak to us on the deck. I use the word "gangway" timorously. I am not at all sure this is the proper term for a narrow aisle that from deck to stern passed, on the outside and on either side of the boat, the staterooms and saloon. I know with certainty it was a passageway nothing on earth would have induced me to use except in an emergency, when I would have sidled like a crab, my back to the water, my front pasted to whatever solid part of the structure I was passing. The crew and Richard used it constantly and nimbly without so much as a finger on the silly low rail along the water side.

Richard told us we were coming into a lock and suggested the towpath between it and the next one would be pleasant for a bicycle ride. Sam was on his feet immediately. After all, he said, he had come on this trip because a bicycle had been promised him. Would anyone like to go along? Albert accepted at once over Frances' protesting reminder of the practice run in Central Park. Albert's answering reminder of who had rescued whom on that excursion silenced her.

"You can keep your eye on the compass," he told her, "in case I go off the towpath." He never said a truer word.

Sam went below, to get his cycling outfit, he said. Two bicycles were lowered over the side. Since we were in the approach to the lock no gangplank was necessary; it was only a small jump down to the flat top of the stone wall that confined the passage. Albert was waiting there, holding the two bicycles, when Sam came back wearing his bicycle outfit. This consisted of a pair of wide rubber bands he assured us had been custom made to enclose exactly his trouser leg around the ankle; bicycle clips were old-fashioned and less efficient. The rest of the outfit was a pair of loose-fitting white canvas gloves with sky-blue knitted wristlets. I had not seen a pair like them since my childhood; they were called then furnace gloves. Frances waved the two adventurers out of sight and returned to her compass. Some time later, perhaps half an hour, with a sharp cry she arrested us in our various occupations. She was standing at the rail and pointed.

"Albert is hurt," she said.

We ran to join her and crowding the deck rail saw Albert lying face down on the ground, Sam seemingly standing over him, the bicycle on its side. Cupping her hands Frances called, her voice quavering, "Is anything broken?"

Albert evidently did not hear her, but Sam straightening up turned to face us.

"Yes," he said, "the bicycle chain." He held up both hands; the gloves were black with grease. He was holding a grisly-looking instrument with a long, sharply pointed end. He grinned.

"The operation was a success," he said, "the patient will recover."

Albert heard this and got to his feet. Pointing to the gloves and the murderous implement, he called as we moved slowly past them: "Always good to travel with a surgeon. He carries his utensils."

We knew the tool was from the kit bag that is part of a bicycle's equipment but we spent some little time in exchanging conjectures about the reason for Sam's choice of "furnace gloves" as a bicycle rider's accessories. I am sure one of us would have elicited the explanation direct from him but we were all distracted by the return of the travelers. Not

so much the return itself as the method. I had spent the inter-
vening time playing a game of Scrabble with Frances. She
had been unnerved by the sight of Albert lying on the
ground, mentioning reasonably that if a wheel should fall off

so would Albert. Our game did not distract her completely.
Sometimes during it she called my attention to the absence of
visible habitations along our route. Even the towpath Albert
and Sam had taken was now out of our sight because of heavy
undergrowth between it and the water.

"In case anyone needed to go for help," she amplified.

Vigorous halloos in male voices brought us to our feet and the deck. The others joined us. The cyclists intact were calling from the bank. They had come into our view some distance ahead of us but David had already sighted them and was nosing the *Palinurus* toward the bank at a spot where an upright heavy iron pole indicated a temporary mooring place. Richard in the bow, a coiled rope in one hand, jumped to the bank as soon as the distance between permitted. He made the boat fast and, on his way toward the stern where David would throw another rope, called over his shoulder to the cyclists as they came toward him he would have the gangplank down in no time.

Like a king about to address his people from a royal balcony Albert raised his arm.

"Don't bother," he said, "we're coming aboard on the boom." Frances, standing beside me, moaned. If Sam's qualifying announcement was intended as a reassurance to Frances it fell wide of the mark.

"We won't carry our bicycles with us," he said. "They can be taken on the gangplank."

Sophy announced she would use it to go ashore, in order to come back on the boom. She was impatient to try it, but the men could come first, she said. Watching them as well as Richard, she would be sure of the technique.

Richard continued on his way toward the stern, caught the rope David flung him, securing it around the trunk of a tree. When he came back to the adventurers he was smiling, almost grinning, and this was unusual. Richard, perhaps because of a constant awareness of his responsibility or perhaps by nature, was a sober young man who permitted very few light moments.

"Give us the boom, David," he called.

When David had obliged, Richard asked the aspiring aerialists if they would like him to go first.

"So that you'll get the hang of it and I'll be on deck to give a hand—if that should be necessary," he added courteously. They gave him precedence with alacrity, perhaps eagerness.

He made an effortless spring from the ground, grasped the boom with both hands and then bent over it. In this position he gave a vigorous backward push with his feet and under the momentum swung slowly and smoothly over the water. The boom, completing an arc, stopped above the deck, to which Richard dropped.

At a push from David the boom moved over the water again and stopped above the place on the bank where Sam and Albert were waiting. They did not toss a coin for the first rider. Albert's deference to seniority seemed heartfelt, even insistent. Sam made the first push off. It was not like Richard's. Richard had leaned over the pole; Sam was doubled over it. By the time he was above the water he was like a man in the throes of a violent attack of colic, knees hunched, legs thrashing. There was no outcry, however; he was a stoic. When his legs stopped churning and his body straightened he was on the deck.

"I think perhaps I bent too far," he said, "or maybe I'm too tall for that boom."

If height was a disturbing factor in Sam's passage, lack of it may have been the cause of Albert's remarkable propulsion. Like Richard he jumped to reach the boom; Sam had scarcely stood on tiptoe, we remembered later. Albert bent over it, gave a backward push with both feet and left the bank. That was where the similarity to Richard's passage ceased. Over the water Albert's stance changed from a bending curve to a stiff perpendicular. From the waist up he became the man on the flying trapeze and from the waist down a six-day bicycle racer, with a difference. A racer covers ground toward his goal. Albert's pedaling brought the boom to a standstill. Its tip was too far from the boat for Richard to reach; there was no physical assistance possible unless perhaps the boom could have been lassoed by a rope and drawn in. Albert did not need this kind of assistance. What brought him to safety, I am

sure, was Frances' message, something between an entreaty and a command.

"Albert," she called, "get back on the boat."

Albert on the instant ceased pedaling, became all trapeze artist. He pulled himself up and over the boom and, pedaling again, set it in motion. David and Richard leaning over the rail put their combined strength to the pole the moment it was in reach and returned Albert to his infuriated wife.

Sophy had not gone ashore. When Richard politely told her it was now her turn, she answered with even more formal politeness she had decided not to hold up our departure for her own pleasure. Perhaps she might try another time.

Albert did not ride the boom again, nor a bicycle. I had a premonition he would not, when he told me that evening, in private conversation, on the ride with Sam he had fallen off four times. Not because of inadequacy as a cyclist, he wished me to understand, but because the ruts on either side of the road were pebbly and therefore very jolting to the seat. Confiding this to Sam, he had been advised to rise in the stirrups, so to speak, but this had necessitated doing more than two things at once, pedaling and steering as well as standing on the pedals, and so he had fallen off. The next suggestion, his own, was that he move from the ruts to the smooth grass along the middle. The grass had turned out not only to be smooth but slippery, so that he had slid down and fallen off first on one side and then the other.

"Fortunately," he said, "it's my seat that took the most punishment. I can still *walk* the towpath."

10

GERTRUDE LAWRENCE, unforgettable in *The King and I,* sang the haunting song "Getting to Know You . . . Day by Day."

Day by day we were getting to know one another in ways years of friendship had not revealed. It was not that we were having what in college we used to call "soul scrapes"; it was that we were living the days slowly and in a proximity that gave opportunity as well as leisure for awareness of tastes, responses, habits—and foibles.

Margalo explained the reason she was the first one up. She could share the crew's breakfast and be out on deck before Jacques returned from the baker's with fresh bread and croissants. I asked her a little enviously what made the crew's breakfast different from ours; I supposed for people who were going to work hard all day a more substantial meal was provided, probably with extra delectables. Crew's breakfast I was told was coffee in cups without saucers.

The order of the day was established early and easily. Neill was the last to come up for breakfast and ate alone. Sophy, Albert and Sam took a walk before their first meal. Returning with hearty greetings and reports of how briskly they had traveled and how beautiful the country was in the early morning, they broke into the happy silence of the others at their respective tables, and were conspicuously ignored. When the temptations that drove Margalo to the deck were reduced to a few crumbs she would reappear to take on tasks she invented in her self-appointed role of Decky. She helped Emma clear away, offered ashtrays all around, with comments in an accent she assured us was appropriate to the part.

When the barge was in motion, traveling a stretch that was impractical for walkers or cyclists, we were almost as scattered as when we went ashore. There were no group activities; we congratulated ourselves, and fervently thanked the Lord for the absence of a single organizer among us. I am not very perceptive, I have been told, but it did seem to me curious that whenever someone made an observation about how pleasant it was that no one said, "Let's do this" or "I suggest everybody go to such and such a place," all those present looked at me, as if they had expected I would be the one to make such proposals.

Sam had begun to surprise Cornelia before they even reached the barge. Learning he was to be a fellow passenger on the *Queen Mary*, she had admitted to Sophy and me a childlike anticipation.

"Imagine," she had said, "going from Cherbourg to Paris with someone who has never seen that country before. Imagine showing Paris. I can picture his face when he steps inside Notre Dame or the Louvre."

There was nothing to picture on his face, she told us later. His expression did not change outside or inside Notre Dame, the Louvre or whatever place they visited. He was polite, acquiescent and totally disinterested. He liked life, he had explained, and music, especially opera. In return for her kindness, wasted she told us, he had taken her to a performance of *Madama Butterfly*. The performance was mediocre but it was after all in the glorious Opéra Comique. Sam was indifferent to the performance and the Opera House. The music, familiar and loved, was there; that was the reason he had come.

We soon learned on the barge how familiar opera music was to him. He sang a good deal of it a good deal of the time, nodding his head to mark the tempo. This urge to sing seemed to come on him unexpectedly, but after the first day we did not jump when an aria exploded. He was fond of poetry, too, and knew an astonishing amount, but he recited more quietly than he sang.

Neill occasionally sang too. The songs were familiar, but to join in was a mistake. Either he did not know or was bored by the middle section. He went immediately from the opening to the closing lines; the joiner floundered between.

On the second night at dinner Sam spoke indignantly of an architectural feature he had become aware of, and disliked. His vehemence startled us because Sam is a most equable man, patient, tolerant, philosophic, benign.

"What is all this business in France of walls?" he had demanded. "High stone walls everywhere closing off houses. What kind of people are they? What do they want to shut themselves away for? What are they hiding? Are they scared? Or are they selfish? Don't they want other people to enjoy their gardens if they have any? Or call 'hallo,' passing by?"

Someone murmured sympathy with a desire for privacy but Sam flouted that point of view.

"I'll accept a man's home being his castle, but that's inside. The outdoors ought to be open to everybody. I'd be very suspicious of people who wouldn't let me look at their outside."

Romney said he would like to put the kind of wall Sam disapproved of around a whole city in order to shut out the countryside and he would stay in the very center of that city and never move from it except to go to another one, though he could never remain long away from New York, after that from Paris, then London.

His dislike was of churches, outside and in. His father, he told us, had been an articulate and determined agnostic; therefore, his son had no association with churches either antipathetic or nostalgic. He recognized but did not warm to their beauty. His responsiveness was to the arts within their own framework. For example, he explained, he did not respond to color in a stained-glass window or in nature, but to its representation by a painter. Like Sam he loved music but preferred the sound of words, and, most of all, performances. He was blissfully happy, he told us, to be in this group of congenial friends, and he loved when we went ashore to hear the French language, but he would shy at entering into a conversation with people he did not know. They might think him intrusive. Sam would begin a conversation with anybody and was never rebuffed.

Albert had arrived in France, we had learned, with a love of French ice cream, but it was on this trip, he told Sophy, he had learned to look at, listen to, and love Nature. He had told her this on one of their before-breakfast walks when, a hand on his arm, she had stopped him, saying, "Listen, Albert, listen. My God, it's a skylark!"

When the song had stopped Albert had turned to her wide-eyed, and said, she repeated later, "I don't believe I've ever before in my life deliberately listened to birds. I've heard them, of course, but I think I've just taken them as part of the countryside. That's what comes I guess of being brought up in the city and in the theatre. I can identify voices pretty well I think—you know accents and all that—but no one has ever said to me, 'That's a robin you're hearing, or whatever.'"

A little farther along in their walk he had amplified, evidently having been brooding over this: "You know, here's a funny thing. All those years Frances and I lived in California I was crazy about our garden. But it must have been something quite separate in my mind from Nature, that is, I mean the countryside. That first day, driving from Orly to Samois, when the rest of you began calling out about those slashes of mustard fields among the green ones, I began to catch on to something different and now I'm looking around all the time. And the things I'm seeing!"

To the group, Brother's preoccupation with a camera was not remarkable, but to me it was as astonishing as Frances's absorption in a compass. Almost from babyhood I knew he had been fascinated by machines, but to attract him they had to be on a large scale like locomotives, or on a lesser one, automobiles. At the age of five he could identify any make of car and over the years his knowledge has widened and his enthusiasm mounted; but I do not remember seeing him with a box Brownie between his hands. On this trip I never saw him without a camera even during meals, and he behaved as if he were on an assignment from *Life* magazine with instructions to cover every object and activity of every day. He photographed trays of food before they were put on the table. I have seen one likeness of the chef's arm but I daresay that was unintentional. During the meal he would leave his place and presently a telltale click would reveal his capture of the unromantic sight of ten people munching. The results have made an album that will be a joy forever, but

I still find it difficult to believe the photographer with an eye for composition, light and shade was my brother.

Of all the passengers there is no question that Neill was the most paradoxical. I am not quite so backward as to visualize

all admirals as Lord Nelsons, always standing on the bridge, feet wide apart to maintain a balance with the rolling seas beneath, a spy glass before one eye. But I would not have supposed that even with the most modern binoculars applied to both eyes an admiral would discover much bird life on his horizon. Furthermore, except for the captain in *Mr. Roberts,* who tended solicitously his potted palm, I have not come upon in literature or life a seafarer with a horticultural bent. Therefore Admiral Phillips' love and knowledge of ornithology and horticulture, while they commanded our respect, shook us. Learning by accident that he is a recognized artist in topiary, we were awed.

When I said some of these things to Brother one day he advised me to talk separately to the Captain and the members of the crew.

"You'll find some surprises there too," he suggested. The suggestion itself did not surprise me. I was ignorant of his attachment to a camera, but I have always known he likes talking to people and finding out about them. It is not a pursuit like Sam's; it seems a more ambling approach, but it gleans knowledge. I told him I'd had in mind learning a little about our host and staff but I might have known he'd be ahead of me.

Since I do not know how to make an ambling one to anything, my approach to Jenny one day, was: "Tell me about yourself. Where do you come from?"

It was a long story, she said, and she would be happy to share it when she had more time. I was changing for dinner at the moment, and she had come in with underclothes she had washed. Eying with disfavor my ablutions in the washbasin, she suggested I take a "proper" bath. The experience brought me knowledge of the barge itself.

A barge except in rate of travel is like other passenger ships. This one, however, had an idiosyncrasy in the bath facilities.

Though I considered the provision of two showers and a tub more lavish than I had anticipated, I had viewed the actual equipment with misgiving. The tub stood so high from the floor it seemed to me only a ballet dancer after long practice at the bar could swing a leg over it. The showers were suspended over a shallow trough lined with tile that looked to me not only glazed but glassy. That was the only reason for my uneasiness. The shower itself was a model I first saw in Greece. I give it such enthusiastic endorsement I have had one installed in my New York apartment. This is a long flexible hose with a spray at the end. In Europe it is called a telephone shower because that is what it looks like when cradled. In use it can be applied and directed by the authority of the bather. I greatly prefer this to the battering-ram assault or the artful dodging required when the shower heads are immovable fixtures.

With the soothing assurances of a nanny, Jenny eased my doubts of keeping my footing on the tile. She said I need not try the tub if I thought I'd get stuck with one leg up in the air, but the shower stalls were safe and beautiful. Like the comment on bathing machines in "The Hunting of the Snark" I considered this "a sentiment open to doubt."

"Sloshing about with a sponge at the basin in your cabin is not good at all," Jenny declared and, quailing under this disapproval, I headed for the shower equipped with sponge, soap and towel. There was a stool in the shower room I had not noticed in my first inspection. I thought if I placed it inside the trough and sat on it I might lessen the possibility of skidding, but a second thought, that the stool itself might skid, prompted me to leave it in place, and, since there was no hook on which to hang them, pile my night-gown, bathrobe and bath towel on top, my bedroom slippers on the floor alongside. I stepped inside the trough and stood firmly, feet a little apart.

The water came on immediately and pleasurably hot. I adjusted the temperature in the manner that is another rec-ommendation for this model. During the adjustment the in-strument can be held away from the bather instead of the bather's having to retreat from a scalding or a freezing, alter-nating with rapid and courageous sorties toward compromise. The proper temperature established, I began an overall sluicing, delicious, soporific, justifying all Jennifer had said.

When the water stopped I had placed the telephone at the nape of my neck in order to hose down my back. For some interval of time I was not disturbed by the absence of water; undoubtedly it was being used elsewhere and would return to me when another shower or tap was turned off. But when a greater time had passed and I was beginning to feel chilled I brought the shower head around to the front, wondering if on this one there was an extra attachment for turning off and on that I had involuntarily manipulated. What I brought around to the front was a full-strength assault into my face at close quarters. There was no absence of water; there never had been. The head itself could be swiveled and in putting it behind me I had swiveled it. The cascade of water diverted from me had been directed with magnificent aim, not of my doing, at the stool that held my clothes and bath towel. On the floor at the moment of discovery, my slippers afloat were bumping against the door sill. Since with this controlled instrument a cap is not necessary, my hair had shared with my face the full drenching. Jennifer was still tidying my cabin when I shouted. She brought a blanket.

Other baths brought more immediate and intimate knowledge of others in our group than years of friendship would have exposed.

A number of us could have heard Frances say she was confined to her shower by a door that stuck, had she called the news. We were in the saloon at the time engaged in various occupations, and when we heard someone whistling, we knew from its direction the whistler was taking a shower in the room immediately below. Many people sing or whistle when they bathe but I did think this was a limited repertory. After the repetition some dozen or so times I hoped presently the artist would consider the fragment practiced enough and move on to another. I was surprised when Albert, sauntering in from the deck, heard it, jumped toward the stairs and down them, calling back, "What's the matter with Frances?"

We learned at dinner the fragment was a family code meaning, "I need help."

When, along with our apologies, those who had heard it chided her for not sending out a message we could have decoded, she told us characteristically she hadn't wanted to bother anyone and was sure Albert would hear her eventually. When she admitted she had whistled for one hour I knew why the phrase had begun to seem to me monotonous. Frances assured us she had not been too uncomfortable, but confessed her mouth felt set in a rosebud pucker she hoped would not be permanent.

Emily reproached me a few days later for not warning her about the swiveling shower head. When she told at lunch of her astonishment at seeing her slippers floating on the surface of what turned out to be ankle-deep water—she had thought the water temporarily shut off—I interjected sympathetically the same thing had happened to me. The admission was a mistake.

"Now you tell me," she said bitterly. "Come after lunch and see my bedroom slippers." I invited her to take a look at mine but she declined.

There was no possibility of misunderstanding Cornelia's message when she called for help. The cries reached up the stairs through the saloon and out to the deck. Since we were moored at the time I daresay a number of French supper-table conversations were enlivened by speculation on the goings-on of the party on board the *Palinurus,* judging from the noise they were making. I do not know why Cornelia had selected the tub, but when I asked her, the experience had turned her a little surly, and I did not press the question. I did learn that by means of a folding kitchen ladder provided

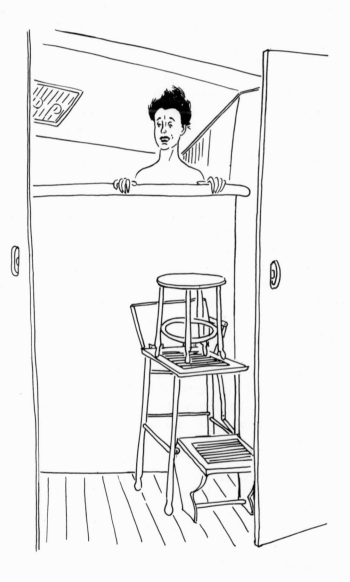

by Jennifer and a footstool from her own cabin on top of this she had been able to get in. She had enjoyed a blissful soak while she contemplated, with somnolent complacency, the craven spirits of her companions who had not dared climb so high. When the inevitable moment for descent arrived, she discovered a wet foot could find no purchase on the smooth surface of the stool and the rim of the tub was too high, since she was not a ballet dancer, to accommodate her foot while she dried it. She tried easing herself in a sitting position from tub to stool but this rocked the entire climbing apparatus, stool and ladder beneath, threatening an overall entanglement on the floor. She might have placed a towel on the smooth stool to provide a purchase, but she had left it out of reach. She sent out a call for help and repeated it at intervals, softly. When she saw she was becoming all-over corrugated from such long immersion, she projected.

All of us responded to what was more a bellow than a clarion call, but Sophy was the first to reach the scene. It is possible Sophy provoked Cornelia's surliness by insisting on fetching a camera from her cabin and, after several shots, returning it for safety's sake before she would extend one helping hand and with the other steady the stool-ladder structure.

Of all the inadvertences that occurred I consider Romney's the fanciest. During a game of Scrabble one evening he apologized for seeming fidgety. Taking pity on my obviously bewildered acceptance of his apology, he conceded a shamefaced explanation.

"I took a tub tonight," he said, "instead of a shower. You've seen how high the tub is, God knows why."

"I've seen it," I told him, "and I wouldn't dream of trying to get into it."

"Well," he said, "not being a tall man I put both hands on the rim and did a sort of vault over and in. Once in I was fine but I didn't realize how low and sloping the overhead is. I finished my bath, took the towel from the rack and stooped over to start drying myself and that's how I got hurt."

I made no comment because the explanation to me still lacked clarity.

"Oh, for God's sake, don't you understand? I burned my derrière on the light. It's very uncomfortable," he added irritably, "but I'll get no sympathy for it. Imagine telling this when I get home. Friends will say, 'Did anything happen to you on the barge trip?' And I say to them, 'Well, yes, I had one accident. I seared my behind on an electric light bulb in the ceiling.' "

SENS was in the full blare of a carnival, a fair and May Day when we arrived at about half past two on Saturday afternoon. We had not needed to be told some such celebration was in progress. We had heard evidence of it at least a quarter of an hour before we docked beside the long quay at the fringe of the town. As my Greek friend Gina Bachauer would say, "everything what you can imagine" was at full volume, carrousels, hawkers, dance-band records—evidently on a number of machines because they played across one another.

Permeating it, a little like a roll of far-off drums, was the sound of people walking and talking, pierced now and then by shrill cries of children. Richard had to raise his voice to make an announcement, though we were all on deck and not far from him. Only part of his news surprised us. The annual fair and carnival were in progress.

We nodded. We had guessed that.

Monday would be the first of May. This we knew. Therefore the locks would not be operated, and since they were open only a half day on Saturday and not at all on Sunday we would remain here until Tuesday morning. We had not anticipated this.

Neill promptly retired to his table of maps and guidebooks. He would chart a course for us, he said, that would make an interesting all-day expedition in the car, perhaps Monday. He paused for a short conference with the General that ended with their agreement to leave the car at Moret for another night since there was no need to hurry back for it. Within a few minutes after Richard's announcement, Neill was the only one left on board. The rest of us went ashore in a group, but characteristically scattered almost immediately. Cornelia had been muttering darkly it was just as she had anticipated, she had not brought the proper clothes. She might find a dress or so here; almost anything would be better than what she had.

This was evidently the day before the actual opening of the fair. Some of the booths were being decorated and their wares unpacked; others were in full operation. Each had its own ballyhooer urging passersby to visit and purchase. Long aisles were filled on either side with booths; there was a separate amusement park and beyond that a space large as a baseball field given over to displays of farm machinery. In the amusement park there must have been twenty carrousels with imaginative conveyances. In my childhood I rode only on merry-go-round horses that either stood still or rose up and down. Here stagecoaches, helicopters, rocket ships, balloons whirled around, but, a pity I thought, very few horses.

The French have gone mad over *le plastique*. I looked at a far greater assortment of kitchen equipment in one booth after another than I would have thought possible in this material, and in an array of dazzling colors that made old sobersides of American manufacturers. *Le plastique* for the French has also overflowed the kitchen to include accessories for every room in the house; I was not tempted by them. I enjoyed looking at the fabrics displayed. There was a marked difference among them of quality but I thought a uniformity of originality and taste in color and design. I did not make a purchase because the "little dressmaker" no longer exists in my home environment, and because the few things I have executed with needle and thread looked like the results of therapy prescribed for a deranged patient.

In the area for children I was beset by an urge to buy, but the still small voice of common sense, to which I seldom listen, persuaded me a charming set of wicker furniture though diminutive in size would have to be shipped, and I have learned how expensive that can be. A four-foot-high white teddy bear with black eyes and an engaging grin could be carried, but not without embarrassment to me and my companions. I moved on.

Reaching the end of one aisle I found I was on the perimeter of the fair itself and on a street leading to the cathedral I could see at its end. The cathedral had been my objective when I left the barge but until the moment of seeing its spire in the distance I had not thought about bringing any head covering. The day was gray, but the sky looked as if the sun might break through. It was cool enough for a topcoat, but I found no scarf in any of its pockets. I need not, however, go back for one.

On either side of me small motor vans lined the curb, making passage slow, and impossible except on foot. The owners of these vans were unloading and displaying, draped over the tailboards, their contents, and these were fabrics. Perhaps this was an overflow from the fairgrounds or perhaps the space was cheaper. I began to shop for an inexpensive scarf, anything that would allow me to observe the convention of entering the church with the head covered. I am scrupulous about this perhaps because I am not a Catholic. I do not like to go into someone's else church with my head uncovered. By the time I had visited the third van I had learned the word for scarf is *foulard,* but had been unable to find one. The stock they carried was bolts of material for curtains and chair covering and these of such spectacular design and luminous color they would have lighted up whatever part of the church I visited, and that was not my intention.

The proprietor of the fourth van I reached was a woman, eager to begin her sales. Certainly she had *foulards* she assured me and of the very best quality. It required only a very small moment of searching. Quality was not important, I told her, only covering, but her head was so deep in a kind of clothes hamper I doubt she heard me. Her vigorous excavation threw up bundles of material. She waded through them toward the interior of the van, calling back to me she would require only a very small instant more. At the bottom of a hamper at the far end, she struck pay dirt. Backing out through clinging heaps of material that made passage difficult, she emerged from the van. Her face was red, her hair disheveled, she was short of breath, but triumphant. In one hand she held a scarf and she waved it triumphantly.

"You see, madame, it is as I told you. One very small moment and I find a beautiful *foulard* of the best quality. And there you see," she thrust it toward me, "just there in the corner the very signature woven into the silk, Bianchini Ferier."

What I had had in mind was not a Bianchini Ferier scarf that cost eight dollars, but I had neither the heart nor courage to dampen her zeal. I bought the *foulard,* tied it over my head and went on to the cathedral of St. Etienne.

The guidebook says the cathedral St. Etienne was the first of the great Gothic cathedrals of France. I say the first sight of its interior made me catch my breath in astonished wonder and blurred my vision with a sudden spurt of tears. I had entered in a moment of involuntary *son et lumière* so overwhelming it lifted my spirit and shook my body. In front of me at the far end of the nave, great windows in deep blue, purple and a translucent green I had never seen before were suddenly set afire by a flash of sunlight. On that instant behind me organ music began and, as I listened trembling, swelled over me, and soared up into the arches. I stumbled forward because I needed to sit down or hold on to the back of a chair, and I crossed the path of Emily coming from a side aisle. Tears were pouring down her face; she did not recognize me until I touched her arm. Her mouth was working; she had difficulty shaping the words she needed to tell me.

"It's César Franck's 'Cantabile for The Great Organ,' " she managed to say. After a few swallows she could shape more words, "I've known that music all my life and I never knew how it was meant to sound. I'm seeing my first cathedral in France, and hearing that music in a cathedral as it was meant to be. My cup runneth over." She buried her face in her hands.

We sat down. Emily, a beautiful pianist herself, had been taught from babyhood by her mother, a musician too and a passionate lover of music, a wide knowledge of the literature of music. I was thinking of that when Emily turned to me, controlled now, though her eyes were still bright with tears.

"I was thinking about—" she began.

I nodded. "I know, so was I. What she gave you and what she wanted for you, and here it is."

We walked. Presently we sat again to look and absorb, and walked again. On our third or perhaps fourth circuit the

Lord blessed our brimming spirits. The sun burst again through the windows, setting all the colors afire and turning one we had noticed least to burning gold. We had been faintly aware that other people had entered the church and were moving about, but at the moment of brilliant sunlight we became more conscious of them because of the absence of movement. On the instant of the gold blaze everyone stood transfixed. I noticed one other thing as we left the cathedral. I had been the only one in it whose head was covered.

The market is across the street from the church. It is a very large circular building with a roof, but the upper part of its circumference is open. Immediately across the threshold we stopped. Colors, movement, and beauty of arrangement transformed this place for selling produce into a vivid, live, mobile composition. Both Emily and I had seen and exclaimed over markets in California but these displays surpassed them. I think I shall never forget the radishes in clusters greater in circumference than my arms could reach. Like old-fashioned nosegays in paper holders these were surrounded by green. The radishes too grow with a white heart so that it is as if one looked at the center of a flower surrounded by pink petals.

An open gallery above follows the rim of the building and makes a second story. We climbed a broad flight of stairs in order to look down on the movement, the displays and the color. Walking round the gallery we were distracted by a stall that offered honey, in more varieties than either of us had seen before. I think I am not exaggerating when I estimate at two hundred or more the number of people in the market at that time, but the only other customer at the honey stall was Sophy. Each of us purchased several jars, choosing some with the comb, some clear liquid, some dark, some light, and some the thick, creamy spread that is my favorite. There were no duplicates.

The weight of our packages discouraged any further sight-seeing and made the return trip longer than we had remembered. Since our departure from the barge, visitors had come into town from all the countryside, and like us were there to see the sights. They moved slowly or not at all and there is no deafness so absolute as a Frenchman's when he does not wish to be disturbed. No "Pardon, monsieur," budges him.

We were very tired and a little irritable by the time we reached the barge. Emma was at the bar to minister to us. I daresay had I crossed a desert I might have been more grateful to come upon an oasis, but not much more than I was to take from Emma's hand a glass of dry Cinzano with ice and a twist of lemon peel. The French call that accessory *un zeste de citron* and zest is what the drink restored in me. The others had preceded Sophy, Emily and me and they had not returned empty-handed. We were scarcely surprised to learn the Hacketts had bought postcards, especially charming they insisted. We were no more surprised that Neill had seen everything the guidebook mentioned and made some discoveries of his own. He had brought back flowers, a plant and some delectable little cakes. We were beginning to suspect, we told him, this was *his* pattern, begun at Samois, repeated at Moret, a return from his periods of vanishment with flowers and sweets.

Sam had explored the town. He had not visited any of the places mentioned in the guidebooks; they did not interest him particularly, but he had talked and talked, learning, he said, interesting things from all kinds of people. Asked if this had taken place in French he raised his eyebrows.

"Of course," was his answer. "How else?"

He had only entered one building. "Very interesting people there," he said, "and I've brought back something too. Look," he pointed to a table. "I visited the market," he explained. "Six jars of honey."

ON Monday the first of May we were still in Sens but not for
long. The afternoon before, Sophy, Cornelia and Neill had
gone by taxi back to Moret and retrieved our car. Finding a
place to park in Sens near the *Palinurus* had taken longer
than the round trip to Moret. With a stopover for the night
at Courlon-sur-Yonne we had been traveling more than a day
and a half. The taxi ride had been under twenty minutes.

The fair was in full blare and color. All the wares were
unpacked and on display, visually and vocally. If there was
a booth that did not have a barker, gramophone, radio or
combination of these we did not find it when we
took an early-morning walk in the town. That anything so
diminutive and unassuming as lilies of the valley could stand
out in this carnival is evidence of their profusion. Those

little flowers are the emblems of May Day and they were everywhere for sale in nosegay bunches two hands would not surround. Tubs two arms could not encircle held the bunches that replenished a vendor's stock. Their perfume was in the air everywhere. Returning to the barge by noon, we found that Neill, whom we had not seen in the town, had brought back a bunch of lilies of the valley so large it required two sizable bowls.

This was the day of the expedition Neill had wrought from his maps and guidebooks. The General at the wheel as usual, we started off. The full strength of the company was encased in the Microbus, Albert and Romney face to face, their legs outstretched on the floor behind the third tier of seats, Frances on the third tier in order to prod Albert from time to time, she said, preventing a stupor from suffocation. Our destination was Troyes, a city only fifty kilometers from Sens. The General drove slowly in order to be able to enjoy with her passengers the gently rolling country of green fields gashed by the blazing tongues of yellow mustard.

We were puzzled by signs on the outskirts of the city that told us we had reached the "agglomeration of Troyes." None of us knew the translation of that word and agreed not to look it up. We preferred to remember we said that we had driven through an agglomeration. At the end of a quarter of an hour's driving we were still in an agglomeration and pronounced the term literal and accurate. Because it was late we had decided to go immediately to a restaurant recommended by the guidebook and begin our sightseeing after we had eaten. We knew the name of the restaurant was the Champagne, an appropriate title since we were in the heart of the champagne country. We knew the name of the street on which it was located but we might have been driving through the maze at Hampton Court, because in spite of whatever direction we headed, we kept returning to the place from which we had started. Overriding repeated sharp requests from the driver either to agree or shut up, each of us pointed and shouted his convictions of the way to go.

When one of the shouters, making himself heard, said the name and pointed to a sign that read "Restaurant Champagne," we were abashed to realize we must have passed it some half-dozen times, less discomfited when Cornelia asked rhetorically how we could have expected to find the best restaurant alongside the railroad station. She returned me to discomfiture, however, not long after. During lunch I was sharing, somewhat loftily perhaps, a bit of knowledge I had extracted from the guidebook and to which I had added an interpretation.

"Troyes, I happen to know, was once known as the city of 'Nightcaps.' It's interesting, isn't it, that the expression should have originated here. Undoubtedly since this is the heart of the champagne country, people drank it the way we would drink milk. So they probably had a last glass before going to bed and began calling it a nightcap."

Cornelia smiled. "There you go," she said, "another rookery explanation. Troyes was called the home of the nightcap because for several hundred years the main industry was the manufacture of the caps people wore on their heads when they went to bed at night. After that went out of fashion they began making stockings and that's their first industry today."

Any further special knowledge or interpretation I might acquire I resolved not to share. Our common knowledge was that Troyes was the city Joan of Arc had promised to wrest from the English and deliver to her king. Granted eight days for this accomplishment, she had ridden in triumph through the gates on the third. Another triumph, when I had come upon its chronicle, had given me delectable pleasure. This was an unusual but successful defense of the city in the sixteenth century. The city was famous then for its little sausages. The invaders could not resist the temptation to sample the delicacies, and evidently the delicacies lived up to their reputation. The enemy fell upon them with such gusto and lengthy enjoyment the defenders were given time to organize a counterattack by which the gluttons were massacred. I had become wary of imparting knowledge; I kept this succulent bit of lore to myself.

The Cathedral St. Pierre et St. Paul built between the thirteenth and seventeenth centuries is magnificent in its size, the richness of its decoration and the glowing beauty of its stained-glass windows, the guidebook says; but if there were a sort of trademark postcard of Troyes, and I am sure there is not, or the Hacketts would have one, it would be of a row of tourists staring at the façade of the cathedral. We made just such a row, gaping in wonder at the complexity, depth and richness of its carving. Inside we all went immediately to a vantage point from which to view from the interior the rose window, overwhelming in size and depth of color, that "pierces," as the guidebook says, the façade.

Coming out of the cathedral we saw there had been a heavy shower. The streets were wet and dotted with puddles, but the sun was shining. We had thought we would walk to other places and for once the group had remained together, but at the sight of the puddles we took to the car and were immediately lost again, this time pleasantly. We were looking for a way back to the agglomeration, and home. Sophy drove around a corner the majority opinion said would lead to the main road. It brought us to a street ahead too narrow for a car. Ignoring puddles, we set out at once to explore the way ahead on foot. Certainly it was Neill who identified it.

"We're at the Street of the Cats," he told us. "I remember the guidebook says and I quote, 'It is picturesque with wooden houses whose corbeled gables almost touch over the narrow street.' I remembered it because I did not know what corbeled gables are. I don't know now for that matter but isn't the street fascinating?"

No one disputed this. A little further on still on foot we came to the rue Champbeaux, where the house fronts displayed crossed timber work (*pans de bois*). One, known as the "goldsmith's turret," flaunted a beautiful turret supported by sculptured consoles.

"We must find the rue de la Trinité," Neill said.

When we had reached it, he led the way to No. 7. I did not appreciate the glee with which my friends received his information about it.

"*This* was the place," he said, "where the hosiery trade began, supplanting nightcaps."

Our pace need not have been so leisurely on the way to Troyes; the return trip to the barge gave us plenty of opportunity to survey the landscape. The traffic to and from Sens was a two-way slow procession. Those people who were not coming to an evening at the fair were leaving it at the end of the May Day holiday to go home. We inched our way into and through the city. The traffic lights and the policemen were of small consequence in the torrent of cars. The strain on Sophy had been heavy, not so much perhaps from the driving itself as from the constant and conflicting advice from her passengers. The result of this helpfulness was a complete circuit of Sens three times before she found the proper and familiar street to the barge.

At dinner, refreshed and revived, we had sufficient grace to admit to Sophy our helpfulness had perhaps been too vocal. Frances said, with unexpected truculence, if the rest of us had kept quiet she could have told Sophy the way at once. Her compass had been in her hand, of course, but she had been unable to make herself heard.

"Sophy," Neill silenced us with a note of authority in his

voice we had not heard before, "a general can't allow back talk. You've got to learn that. When I'd been at Annapolis two weeks, my old nurse Martha stopped Mother on the street one day to ask how I was doing. Mother said, 'Fine.'

" 'Well,' Martha told her, 'maybe take him another week or two to get to be a Ad-*mi*-ral.'

"You've got another week, Sophy, to get to be a general who says, 'Shut up!' " "

Sophy beamed. "Watch me."

A measure of her fatigue was Sophy's admission next morning. She had gone blissfully and immediately to sleep, lulled by a full-strength cacophony from the fair that had kept the rest of us awake and with teeth on edge until well after midnight.

13

WE left Sens without Sophy and Neill aboard. They were going to take the car to Joigny, where we were scheduled to moor for the night. Overhearing this plan Richard had said we would come to the town of Villeneuve by twelve o'clock. He suggested they bring the car that far, rejoin us on the barge for the afternoon and return from Joigny to pick it up.

They were waiting for us at Villeneuve, and we paused only long enough to pick them up, not, however, by way of the boom. Several of us at the rail welcoming the motorists urged them to seize this opportunity to swing over the water. We directed our proposal especially to Sophy, but accepted without comment her unqualified refusal She said it would hold things up, an obscure statement, I thought. We let it pass. The General knew she had not fooled anybody with her excuse, and this rankled. To turn away from any challenge was a new and unpleasant experience for her. I could not have known her since I was eighteen and not recognize these traits. This is how I knew she was laying it on at lunch about the beauty of Villeneuve and her regret the rest of us had not been privileged to see it. Neill echoed her praises, but I thought he seemed a bit dazed by their warmth.

"The most beautiful medieval town," she said, "with a fascinating pair of gateways. There was a charming eighteenth-century post house called the House of Seven Heads, and a handsome church."

They had had a drink at Le Dauphin—wonderful provincial atmosphere. Some fishermen had come into the bar for a glass of wine. They had stood, foot on the rail, talking about the day's catch.

"The best part of all," she reached the climax, "there were no other tourists there or in the whole town." She smiled at the rest of us, whose presence would have made a jarring intrusion.

Sometime in the afternoon I heard Emily tell our Captain it was too bad we had missed Villeneuve and pushed on to Joigny.

"I never thought of it," he told her. "It's a nice little town, nothing extraordinary."

We reached Joigny at about half past four in the afternoon, and docked in the town at a long quai. Across a broad, cobblestoned street we saw a café and a line of shops. Emily, Cornelia and Brother volunteered to hire a taxi and go back to Villeneuve for the car, to spare Sophy and Neill a second trip. They would telephone for a taxi from the café over the way. I think Emily still felt from Sophy's description she had missed a treasure. Sophy yielded to their insistence with fairly good grace. I suspect she was a little discomfited by their projected visit to the paradise she had described.

Though the day had been sunny, at the moment of their leaving, clouds gathered and spilled a shower. The volunteers were not to be put off, they insisted, by such unimportance; moreover, Cornelia said happily, for once she had the proper equipment for an occasion. She would put it all on. The equipment turned out to be a raincoat, no special footwear, and she had not thought to purchase a rain hat. She borrowed mine and it became her so well I did not have the use of it until our barge trip was over. She wore it also, at a jaunty angle, as a sun hat.

Impatient to see the town, Sophy and I, after waiting a quarter of an hour for the rain to stop, left the barge. We ran across the wide street to the row of shops, whose overhang gave some protection. Though I wore a raincoat, I had no hat. Later, under the compulsion of a guilty conscience, Cornelia told me she, Emily and Brother were in the café when Sophy and I had darted across the street and passed it. Further admission was that at the sight of us all three of them had ducked their heads instantly and involuntarily under the table. Cornelia said Emily even put her hands over her face and turned her back to the window. Cornelia wanted less to see than be seen by me, because, she explained, had she looked at me in the rain, she would feel she must relinquish my hat; she did not wish to do this. She shared with the others another reason for ducking us. When there had been no answer to Brother's telephone call from the café to the taxi stand, they had thought it a good idea not to rush things, but as long as they were in an obvious place for it, have a drink and try the telephone number later. At the sight of Sophy and me, however, they had felt like children sent on an errand and caught dallying.

Sophy and I, unaware of the proximity of these truants, stayed as close as possible to the shop fronts. We went into one shop to make some small purchases, postcards among them, since Frances and Albert had started an epidemic. When we came out the rain had stopped. We moved away from the shelter and the shopping street and began to explore the town itself. The guidebook defines Joigny as a busy, picturesque little town, "set at the gateway to Burgundy on the borders of the forests of Orthe. It is built in terraces on the side of St. James Hill overlooking the River Yonne."

Terraces are not what I would call the almost perpendicular ascent to the church of St. Thibault, the Church of St. John and the old houses. We labored up narrow winding cobblestone streets made slippery as glass by the recent rain, and a hazard in the best weather, because motorists gathering speed for the ascent did not allow their cars to be slowed by silly pedestrians in their way. I startled more than one householder by lurching through his open doorway, a car in such close pursuit I could feel on my posterior the draft its passage created.

The wooden gate at the extremity of the town has a squat round tower on either side. The guidebooks say the gateway was built in the twelfth century and was once part of the old castle. Within a few minutes of viewing it I wished I had stayed in the protection of its towers. They would have provided a support against which I would have attached myself like a plaster. The way down, since it was by the same streets, was as steep as the ascent had been, the stones as slippery. The only difference is that to slip on the way down is to slide further. Reaching a corner of the church of St. Theobald I pressed a hand flat along the stone exterior. My palm stung and was cut a little, but I was able to stop, and then sidle round a corner and through the doorway. Sophy was ahead of me, and from the threshold held out an arm I grabbed thankfully.

The church was not spectacular but for us it was a haven

we were glad to occupy for a few minutes. While I caught my breath and rubbed the calves of my legs I watched a group of small children come sedately from a side chapel where I supposed they had been at a confirmation class. The little girls and some of the little boys wore blue or black coverall aprons with long sleeves I thought had gone out of fashion years ago. They walked demurely except for one boy who was inclined to cavort and prance but was reclaimed to propriety by the frowns and headshaking of his companions. The instant the threshold was crossed a wind of shouts and squeals blew into us the same tone and volume that can be heard outside any American school at recess time. Long sleeves, black aprons do not throttle the vocal chords.

The same guidebook that told us we had climbed terraces says, "The tourist who likes to stroll along the narrow streets, round the church of the St. Theobald and St. John, will find old dwellings with wooden walls dating from the 13th, 15th and 16th centuries."

We found the old dwellings and exclaimed at the overhanging cross-timbered upper stories, but we did not stroll, and some of our exclamations were directed at motorists who passed us barely. As we gingerly rounded a turn, the sight ahead and not far below, of the level street, the quai and the *Palinurus,* was as beautiful to us as anything we had seen on the heights. Safely there, still upright and only slightly mud-spattered, we met Frances and Albert out for a stroll. We told them what we had seen and how it had been. They thought they would try a little of it. On their return they assured me I had not exaggerated. During one slide Frances admitted she had found herself unexpectedly in a tango position with Albert and together they had done a few swooping turns.

Emily and Cornelia, Brother at the wheel, brought the car alongside the barge shortly after we had gone aboard. They would have got back earlier, each assured the company, had the rain not made it so difficult to find a taxi that was free. Brother, because he is always interested in such things, had timed the trip from door to door. It had taken exactly twelve and a half minutes. The *Palinurus* had required four and a half hours.

Romney, Sam, Sophy and I immediately left the barge to make a short tour by car of the countryside; Neill of course had not been seen from the moment we had docked. Sophy urged Brother to stay at the wheel but supported my plea to stay away from the town and its "terraces." Brother eyed her skeptically.

"I'm with Emily this time," she told him. "I know she's a little demented in a car, but these drivers are lunatics and the streets are glass."

"If *you* say so," was Brother's answer, "we're for the countryside."

Had he not acceded, I would have climbed out of the car. I wish I had climbed out. We went to the Hill of St. Jacques. As Sophy and Brother had agreed, I am a craven in a car; also I hate heights. The guidebook states clearly the ride we took. I had not previously read the passage. It says:

"The road climbs in hairpin [*hairpin,* mark you] bends round the hill of St. James. During a bend to the right, there is a fine semi-circular panorama over the town and the valley of the Yonne." I did not see it. I was sitting on the floor of the Microbus with my eyes shut.

For me, the most beautiful sight on my two excursions in and around Joigny was the *Palinurus.*

_14_

BETWEEN Joigny and Auxerre there are nine, perhaps ten, locks. Warning us this would make a long day of travel, Richard had told us the night before we would leave at nine in the morning. Since the first night when the crew had dined with us, the Captain had not been in our vicinity long enough for any conversation. If we were on deck when we approached a lock we would see him always on the run from stern to bow and back again, casting the ropes, drawing them in again. He would call out a phrase or so of information, comment on or answer a question from one of us. He used the time when we were in the locks to talk with the man or woman operating them. Jennifer had told me he was respected and liked everywhere on the waterways. He spoke their language, she had said, in more ways than just French, and so they passed on to him the news they had of river and canal affairs. It was Jennifer too who had told me the reason we saw more women than men operating the locks: though a lock keeper was given a house rent free, his pay came to only about $45 a month. Therefore, he usually supplemented this by working on the roads, which the regulations permitted him to do, turning over to his wife the operation of the gates. When I had asked her why we saw so little of Richard between locks, she told me it was because the mountain of paper work he had to do kept him hard at it in his cabin whenever David did not need his help.

Coming into the saloon for a book on the morning we left Joigny I was understandably surprised not only to see Richard sitting at one of the tables there but drinking a glass of beer. I had not supposed he ever sat down, I told him, except at his desk. I would have pictured him even eating his meals standing or running. He agreed ruefully, it was an unusual sight, explaining he had been told at the last lock we would be delayed at the following one by boats ahead of us, so he was taking advantage of it. I asked if I could take advantage of his advantage by asking him things about the boat and himself I wanted very much to know. He told me he was not much good at talking about himself but he did enjoy telling about the *Palinurus*. That was a good place to start, I suggested, because I was curious about the choice of names. From reading Virgil a century ago more or less, I remembered the story of Palinurus, Aeneas's pilot who was lost at sea. Was it a vengeance of the gods for Aeneas's betrayal of Dido? Or had he thrown himself overboard? How else had he managed to carry the rudder away with him or had he simply gone to sleep and fallen overboard?

"That's it," Richard broke in, "that's the fellow. When I bought the barge I was reading *The Unquiet Grave* by Cyril Connolly writing as Palinurus, and I was wondering if some of the things he said about that pilot applied to me, wanting to get away from places and things. I don't think so now, but that was why I named the boat."

There was a copy of the book on a shelf in the saloon. I took it to bed with me that night and found, I think, the passage to which Richard had referred. It reads, "Palinurus clearly stands for certain will-to-failure or repugnance-to-success, a desire to give up at the last moment, an urge toward loneliness, isolation, an obscurity."

Saying the word "Palinurus" accomplished for me what "open sesame" did for Ali Baba. Richard opened and without other fumbling questions from me talked of himself and his boat. He had grown up near Wolverhampton and could not remember a time when he had not been drawn to the English waterways. He had been sent to Marlborough, an English public school, had gone one year to the University of Reading, left that to go into the Navy, left that at the end of two years, got a job on a provincial newspaper. He had bought a canal boat—the English call them narrow boats—and lived on it.

"I still own it. David and Jennifer lived on it last winter." He was well into his story now.

"I had rather large ideas that stories I wrote about the canals for the newspaper would help keep them open, and the Inland Waterways people did give me encouragement. I know now I was trying to keep the canals open for *me*, so that *I* could live away from towns, be independent." I remember his grin when he added, "If I had lots of bills I could move. Then I decided to give up the job on the provincial newspaper. I thought I still wanted to be a reporter. If I learned another language and more about the overall political scene I thought I could get a better job, so I came to Paris and studied at the Sorbonne. That was a mistake too. It wasn't what I wanted at all, except learning the language was a good idea. I went every weekend somewhere on the water, got lifts on barges, came to know the owners of companies that operated them, walked the whole of some canals out of use. I wanted to see why and where they started and where they ended. It finally came to me this was what I really wanted. After that I kept looking for a barge I could own.

"The day I saw this boat I'd only a ruler with me but I took its dimensions with that. When I got home I doodled a bit with them, then presently had some plans. Then I went back to London, got prices on everything and showed the plan and the prices to my brother. He's a businessman, luckily for me. He doubled the prices automatically and said he'd put some money in it with me. I was still working for Reuters, going back and forth from England to France. Then one day I found a man I knew could build or rebuild my boat, I can't imagine why. When I saw him he was sitting alongside a canal, as a matter of fact not too far from here. He looked older than sixty-three that I found out later was his age. He was about as dirty as any man I've ever seen, shirt, trousers and face, but we had a drink together in a little café and for some reason I began to tell him about my plans. He said he could carry them out and I believed him. He said, 'Donnez-moi un pied sur la terre et je peux lever le monde,' and you know the fellow actually could. He'd find a way of doing what needed to be done and what seemed impossible. He didn't own a boatyard, only a slipway, but that day in the café I said he was my man. I wired my brother. He took my word for it, God knows why, very decent of him, put up the money he had promised and in July I bought the canal boat I had measured."

Richard paused, smiling reminiscently. "That was a day," he said. "We blew ourselves to a bottle of champagne that night, the old fellow and I."

I prodded a little. "When did you start work on it?"

"We scraped and scoured the rest of the summer. It seemed like years. I moved in at the start. Gave up my job with Reuters. Took over the cabin you have now. A bed and a stove were the first things I bought. In no time I was as dirty as the old fellow himself"—Richard never called him by name, always the old fellow. "The boat had been a coal barge. We had to scrape through layers of coal dust accumulated for years. I probably carried enough coal dust on me to have fired a boiler. I think that's what gave me the idea of turning it into a passenger boat. I'd thought I only wanted to live on the barge and operate it but I knew I never wanted to see another load of coal or cargo of any kind again once my barge was clean." He shuddered.

"So the rebuilding began?" I repeated.

"Sometime in September. The old fellow had hired all the workmen, welders, carpenters, electricians, local people. They hadn't a clue of what I wanted—I was rather vague about it myself—but they knew their own jobs. Nobody made mistakes. Nothing had to be undone. They had never seen anything like this; neither had I. I think we went on faith. I did know a pleasure boat would require deck space and a saloon and this would mean a higher superstructure than commercial barges carry. Therefore we'd be riding higher than they, especially without cargo. So unless we had a heavy ballast we'd never get under the bridges. We put in eighty tons of concrete and what a job that was. We had to distribute it to keep the balance and compensate for the parts of the boat that would be lighter, heavier, higher, lower. We worked all winter and it was rather brutal. I hope I never will be so cold again—or dirty."

I gave another little push. "When were you actually finished?"

"The digging, cleaning, demolishing and the ballast took so long and cost so much the rest of it seemed to take no time at all. Cabins, saloon, galley, plumbing, wiring and furniture. It was finished, I was ready to start. All I needed, I thought, were passengers. I was very much mistaken. I needed papers.

"To the French, papers mean everything from licenses to other permits, to customs, to refusals. Papers mean a dam built across whatever you wish to do and whatever way you plan to take. Of course I had applied for all the things I knew were required but the administration balked. 'A floating foreign hotel?' Impossible, unheard of, therefore it did not exist. When the administration woke up to the fact that it was true, that I was ready to start, and that I was without regulation, the authorities produced a new reason to refuse credentials. 'A foreigner cannot own a French boat. It is not allowed.' I got around that one by registering my boat in England. The French then asked, 'How did this boat get into France?' That was a difficult question to answer. I did not know what to do and in such cases I do think the best thing is to do nothing. And that is what I did. Nothing. Finally the Commissaire de Tourisme in Paris became interested. And at his recommendation the bureau made what they called 'arrangements.' When the arrangements had been satisfactorily completed, again we were ready to travel. This was when I was told neither David nor I qualified as a licensed pilot. Of course David was licensed, but it was not a French license. It was necessary to engage one. We did engage one and this turned out to be a splendid idea because his wife came along and she knew every bakery and baker from Dunkirk to Dijon. Having got this knowledge we let the pilot go at Dijon and heard no more of the matter. I decided to follow the same procedure in anything else required. When I was told I must have the boat surveyed for a license to carry passengers I was unable to find anyone sufficiently interested to make the survey. And so I let the matter drift. I've heard nothing further about it."

"I suppose there was finally a first trip or I wouldn't be here now," I said.

"The 15th of April, I doubt I shall ever forget that date. You know David and I have been friends since we were boys and I started messing around the canals. So of course he knew about my boat. When I asked him if he'd go in on it with me, he said that's just what he'd been hoping for. He was going to get married, he added, but that wouldn't take long, and Jenny was keen to come along. She'd do beds and whatever. They were married on the sixth and on the tenth they joined me. We had two major stops on that first run.

"The first one was because of the old fellow's only mistake —and it was splendid—he had put on the propellers backward. The second stop was because for no apparent reason and out of the blue, customs people came aboard and refused to allow us to keep the things we had bought in England. They were specialized things for yachting and you can only find them in England: special cookers, blankets, all sorts of things."

I asked how on earth he'd got around that one. Richard smiled disarmingly. "By arrangements," he said.

"So now finally you were on your way?"

Richard nodded. "On our way," he repeated, "without passengers.

"In June and July we had not a single request although my brother had written a brochure and sent it out to the news- papers. So, we cruised the canals. We checked on itineraries that we'd already sent out; we had to make sure the timing was correct. It was a way of getting to know the lock keepers too and all the people along the waterways. So it wasn't wasted, but I was anxious."

I asked what had turned the tide.

"The London *Sunday Times,*" was his answer.

"Someone on the paper picked up one of the brochures,

wrote a piece about it and the inquiries started. In August we had our first passengers and from then on," he knocked on the table three times, "it's been full. We sell individual places, you know, during the season from June to September. The usual tour is for a week but individual bookings can be made for longer. Out of season we only let the barge as a whole, the way you've taken it, and that's the way I'd like to see it hired eventually."

I ventured to ask his far-off plans and we came back to our starting point.

"I'm like Palinurus," Richard said, "I know I'm committed to this. Only something from the outside—I mean administration or money, in other words, the gods—can stop me."

I interrupted to ask when Joachim now called Jacques had been added to the crew.

"There's an organization," Richard explained, "called 'Sopexa.' It has to do with introducing to foreign countries French agricultural products, cooking, wines, all sorts of things. They told me about Joachim. He was working then at the Great Northern Hotel in London. I went to see him, talked about the boat, took him on his day off to see it, and he never went back; not even to pick up his chef's cap."

There was a shout from David outside, "Gate's opening."

Richard jumped to his feet.

"It was all very simple," he called over his shoulder. He was on the run again. "I am committed to water."

15

WHEN Richard had made his announcement about our early start from Joigny, he had added the information that we would remain in Auxerre from Wednesday until Friday. He had smiled across at me.

"You remember," he said, "Auxerre is the place where I suggested you could use your car. I'm glad you didn't wait."

It was a generous admission.

When he had left, Albert, at a signal from Frances, joined her in a corner of the room. They held a whispered consultation. At the end of ten minutes or so, with the solemnity of a delegation, they "waited on" Sophy. Unabashed, the rest of us watched and listened. Something momentous, I felt uneasily, was about to be announced; probably they were going to end the cruise, they had had enough.

Frances was their spokesman.

"Sophy," she said, "would you think it awful if we took the car to Auxerre? Leaving at nine, we would be there in half an hour, and I can have my hair washed. We need to get some money, too, and do a little shopping."

My apprehension must have been shared, because hearing this, a full chorus, as if on cue, called in joyous unison, "Postcards?" There was no antiphonal response from Mr. and Mrs. Hackett.

We waved them off next morning, Albert at the wheel, Frances holding the compass squarely on her lap. Since he is an experienced driver, Albert had not thought to ask Sophy about the possible idiosyncrasies of the car and Sophy, so accustomed to it, did not think to tell him the reverse gear in a Volkswagen is a little tricky, requiring a firm almost a violent hand. I should have told him about the first day Sophy backed a Microbus.

We were in Lisbon on the main thoroughfare at five in the afternoon. From the position into which we had got ourselves, it was impossible to go forward and not plunge into the Tagus River. At that moment of need Sophy discovered she could not shift into reverse. We were addressed in various degrees of emphasis by drivers of cars behind and on either side of us, none of them friendly. Sophy, red in the face, struggled with the gearshift, at the same time returning to the hecklers comments that were, mercifully, audible only to me. When she unexpectedly rose to a crouching position and pounded with both fists the knob of the shift, I did not know whether her purpose was to demolish as much of the machine as she could lay hands on, or express her fury, and she, afterward, was not very clear about what her purpose had been. I think her actual accomplishment was a surprise to her, though she would never admit it. The gearshift slid into reverse. And from that time on, though two fists were not employed again, a heavy hand was used for backing.

Albert's nature is milder than Sophy's. He would have pounded only if she had advised it. Fortunately, when Albert discovered he could not put the car in reverse, the situation was not so critical as ours in Lisbon. He was able to make a wide turn instead. However, the discovery had been made early in the day and it had become increasingly difficult to find parking space that would allow wide enough berth for circling when the time came to move on. We learned all this when, after a long search at the place specified for our rendezvous in Auxerre, Neill, Sophy and I had grown apprehensive. Before their departure, Richard had told them exactly where we would moor, alongside the quay, he had said, at about seven. Frances, whose conscience always hangs heavy, heavy over her head, had assured him they would be at the spot no later than five in case, by some chance, we should make better time than had been estimated.

We found them eventually and they had been there since five o'clock, at a spot a good half mile from our mooring because, Albert explained, "there were no trees." If he were to drive again he could make a wide sweep, since he could not back. They had not in the least minded the wait, they said. Frances had found a hairdresser in the morning. They had done some shopping and spent the rest of the time exploring beautiful things to see.

Sophy, taking over from Albert, demonstrated her modified pounding technique for backing, and brought the car to a parking spot directly opposite the barge. Leaving it there we went on foot for a taste of the town. Although it was late, Frances and Albert describing its charm had so whetted our appetites we could not wait until the next day. They felt a proprietorship, Frances said, because they had seen it ahead of us; they wanted to show the sights. I asked if they were not tired. A little, Albert admitted, but Frances assured him he was not.

We mounted a steep flight of stone steps that turned out to be only a preliminary climb. Every street that branched off from the one we followed was narrow, winding and steep. Shops were closed but their windows were inviting. Sophy, Frances and I loitered; Albert and Neill moved along, of course. When they summoned us with a commanding whistle and bellow, we moved guiltily and fast into the street itself. The sidewalk was too narrow and crowded for rapid walking, the street was narrow too; other pedestrians had spilled into it. Cars moved in single file. Our view ahead was blocked; we did not see Albert and Neill until we had reached them, nor the astonishing tower under which they waited. The street passes under it, like a river flowing beneath a bridge. The bridge is the clock tower, gaudily magnificent, with two great dials, one for the hours, the other for the movements of the sun and moon. The guidebook does not verify this, but I carry a vivid memory of color—both dial faces a madonna blue, the hands and ornamentation gold. The clock itself, according to the guidebook, was installed in the seventeenth century, the tower dates from the fourteenth and was originally part of the town's fortifications.

We counted this a thoroughly satisfactory punctuation mark to our excursion and returned downhill to the barge. Somewhere we lost Neill—we found it unusual that he had been with us as far as the tower—but we gathered on our way other members of the group, each maintaining, characteristically, what he had seen was far and away the best feature of the city—what a pity the rest of us had gone elsewhere.

The view from the barge, however, at the moment we reached it, brought everyone to an agreement he would not have wished to be anywhere but at that spot. A bridge of arches through one of which we would pass when we left Auxerre had been turned by the setting sun to burning copper with a reflection so vivid and so exact of that still evening, each arch was completed under the mirrored surface of the river. Instead of looking through arches, we were seeing what appeared to be closed curves, ellipses like a procession of giant transparent eggs, the river shimmering through and beyond them. As if this were not enough to disturb one's breath, there were swallows darting and skimming all around us. Each one as it crossed and recrossed the path of the sun turned to a flash of gold. Sometimes there were ten, perhaps twenty, flashes simultaneously, and then a string of them like the showers from a Roman candle. We watched until the birds and the bridges were dark, and dined very late.

Sometime before eight o'clock the next morning, I walked to the cathedral. An excursion proposed by Neill the night before and arranged by the General had included the stipulation that we meet at eleven o'clock at the car. We would assume those who did not turn up had decided not to make the trip to Vézelay, where we would lunch and spend the day.

Margalo and Romney at the outset decided not to go. They would prefer, they said, to poke about in Auxerre. Sam reserved his decision. If he was going we would find him at the car. I would be at the car, but I enumerated to myself, with a little smugness perhaps, the number of things I would already have done and seen, because I would be so enterprising and make such an early start. There were several members of our group already inside the cathedral when I reached it. Others came in shortly after. I think the whole company was there but I was too disgruntled to count.

The Cathedral St. Etienne is glorious in the Flamboyant style and the more Flamboyant the style the more I glory in it. The church, built between the thirteenth and the six-

teenth centuries, has two buttressed towers that flank the façade. The façade itself contains four stories of arcades, topped
by gables. The interior is almost overpowering in the majesty
of its size and the range of color in the rose windows.

From there I went alone to see the abbey church of St.
Germanus and its remarkable crypts, that date back to Caro-
lingian time. Then I wandered through the town, stopping
to buy for my granddaughters, in the shop where I had seen
them displayed the evening before, two pairs of charmingly
costumed dolls. I was at the appointed rendezvous at eleven.
Sophy and Cornelia were inside the car. They have been my
dear friends for a very long time and I am still irritated by
their always being ahead of whatever time they have set, making me, precisely on time, feel I ought to apologize for tardi-
ness. It is my contention that Cornelia, on tour, could just as
well take the train or plane that precedes the one on her
schedule since she's sure to be already at the airport or railway station.

At ten minutes past eleven, Sam was the only one of those
planning to go who had not arrived at the Microbus, our
trysting place. We accepted this as his decision to stay behind
and set out, a troupe of eight.

The approach to Vézelay itself is dramatic and unlike any
other on the trip. Long before we reached it we saw the city
high above us like a crown on the brow of a hill that itself
topped the landscape.

A craven about heights, I tend to make an ascent unpleasant for the other passengers. On this one, however, the curves
were broad and the promised land above so inviting I looked
neither out nor down but up.

Unexpectedly we were over its rim and onto a broad flat
plaza. The name of this, according to the guidebook, is the
Champ-de-Foire. On its far side we spotted immediately a
sign reading, "Hôtel de la Poste et du Lion d'Or." Here be-

fore us was the restaurant Alice Lee Myers, an old friend, had told me weeks ago in New York we must be sure to patronize. A meal there, she said, is almost as important as to see Vézelay itself. The General, knowing it was unnecessary to ask our vote on eating or sightseeing first, drove immediately to a space in front of the restaurant and parked the car.

The restaurant is all Alice Lee had promised. We had apéritifs on the terrace that overlooks the square. The day was sunny but, at that height, windy with a chill in the air. We were glad to be called inside when the lunch we had ordered over our drinks was ready.

I do not remember what each of us had for an entrée except Emily, who had snails, the first she had ever tasted. I remember her selection because Neill, watching her, said: "I will never forget the expression on your face, when you tipped the first snail into your mouth, and now, sopping up the garlic butter with a piece of bread. I saw the same expression when you looked at your first rose window—a mixture of awe and ecstasy."

The beginning of the meal I remember too because on our return to the barge when I told about the day to Margalo and Romney I described the dish:

"It was entirely of raw vegetables," I explained, "carrots, cauliflower, celery, radishes, green peppers, tomatoes, cucumbers, very crisp and cold, no dressing on it but a choice of sauce, either a kind of Russian dressing or oil and vinegar. It was so pretty to look at, too. I'm going to do it at home. It's called *crudités assorties*." And because a literal translation is irresistible to me, I added, "Assorted crudities."

Romney echoed the phrase ruminatively: "Assorted crudities," he said. "It sounds like dialogue written by Albee."

I think of that whenever the dish is on my table and it is there frequently.

We went in the car from the restaurant to the basilica on a one-way street that is as close to perpendicular as I think a car can manage. Once we had reached the summit we left the car separately, as usual, and did not return for a very long time.

The basilica physically is a restoration, a triumphant accomplishment by Viollet-le-Duc, according to plans found in ancient documents; its history began in the ninth century. A recruiting ground for the Crusades and a shrine for pilgrims, it contained the relics of St. Mary Magdalene. The pilgrimages fell off somewhat about the end of the thirteenth century when other relics of St. Mary Magdalene were discovered at St. Maximin in Provence. However, the passage of time erased this ambiguity and today in July there is a great pilgrimage to the church and once more the Franciscan fathers are in their monastery.

The guidebook says the nave of the basilica is 203 feet long. I am unable to visualize size in terms of numbers. If I am told something is thirty feet high I endeavor to see five men each six feet tall, and each standing on the head of the one beneath him, but the picture is not clear. Therefore, to read that this nave is 203 feet long means little to me, but I can visualize very well the nave itself because when I stood inside the great doors, my sight traveling the length of it, I felt as if I were looking into infinity. Behind me I heard a breath drawn in as sharp as a whistle. I recognized it even before I turned my head to see. Brother and Cornelia had come through the doors.

"God Almighty," I heard him whisper. Cornelia shook her head slowly and in wonder. "Almighty God," she answered.

By figures, other naves are longer, but this is the one I shall always visualize in my memory.

Behind the church an *allée* of trees is all that remains of the Abbey Palace that was there in the eighteenth century, but below the terrace on which they stand, the panorama of the whole countryside spreads as wide as it did when pilgrims, still far away, looking up could see the great building that housed the shrine toward which they plodded.

When finally we all met at the car we immediately divided again, some choosing to walk down. I was one of those. The way is winding and steep but rewarding: beautiful vistas through arched gateways, old houses, mullioned windows, an antique shop with a charming patio in front and a doorway almost smothered by as beautiful wisteria as I have ever seen, and in full bloom. At the bottom of the street I was following, within a few yards of the square, I saw Emily and Brother leave the window of a shop to go inside. I followed them and once more that day was visually struck by an impact of beauty. We were in a photographer's shop. The pictures round the walls ranged in subject from figures and architectural details in the basilica to horses running in a field, and in size from under a foot to three feet across. A woman was in charge and after a few minutes' conversation, aware of our genuine admiration, she indicated a man sitting shyly in a corner behind a long table that displayed other photographs. In such a dramatic exhibition he would not have been noticed.

"It is my husband," the woman said. "It is he who makes the pictures."

"May I ask your name?" I asked as we shook hands.

"Pierre Kill," he answered. I shall remember that name. I hope one day I shall see his pictures again.

It was hard for them to make a choice but finally Emily and Brother agreed on two.

As we left, Frances and Albert came from a shop across the street. Frances called to us. "The loveliest postcards we've seen anywhere."

At the car, the three Kimbroughs made a declaration. We would not set foot in it, we said, until everyone had seen the exhibit of photography we had just left. There was a good deal of demurring about having to get back and being tired, with acute cases of sight-seeing legs. We held our ground. When we finally drove away, Neill had had to be summoned from the shop by two delegations endeavoring to persuade him to leave without further purchases.

Sam was reading in the saloon when we came on board. Margalo and Romney were playing solitaire individually back to back. We interrupted them ruthlessly. We asked rhetorically if they would like to hear about Vézelay. We had no intention of being prevented from telling them. At the end of everyone's contribution to the narrative, Frances, with characteristic politeness, asked if the stay-at-homes had had a pleasant day. Sophy was already apologizing to Sam. She had been uneasy all day, she said, lest he had meant to join us, had been unavoidably delayed and arrived at the car after we had gone.

Margalo and Romney had had a lovely day, they said, taking a leisurely walk around the town, doing a bit of sightseeing and enjoying a lunch in a restaurant they urged us to visit. It could stand comparison with the best anywhere, with no crudities, Romney asserted, in its menu.

We were scattering to change for dinner—a very small change, we agreed, because we were tired, when Albert thought to ask Sam about his day. Sam was visibly pleased. His eyes lighted up; he put his book aside to make gestures with his hands.

"Wonderful," he said, "wonderful. I found a hospital; beautiful hospital. I asked the porter to take me to a surgeon. He brought me to Dr. Benard, one of the most remarkable men I've ever met. We had a fine conversation about a compound fracture and went over X-rays of it together. He took me to his house for lunch. Beautiful house filled with treasures, and what a garden! The garden is his relaxation and recreation. Of course, a man as busy as he, has to have some quiet and privacy. It's a very necessary thing. So he has a very high wall all around his place. The garden is in front with some beautiful pieces of sculpture set about in it—some of them his; he does that too. And there is a great cage of birds. He is a fine ornithologist as well. So you see, a man like that can't have people walking along the street looking in on him. A wall is a very necessary protection."

No one denied this. No one reminded Sam of earlier observations about walls. We begged him to tell us what more he had done.

"Had a delightful lunch," he said "delicious food of a quality not to be found in any restaurant." He had met the doctor's wife, a charming woman, and a son who had been interesting too and very kind.

Sophy asked if he had gone back to the hospital in the afternoon.

He had not, Sam told us, because the doctor had a busy schedule and Sam had not wanted to impose further on his time. So, at the doctor's suggestion, the son had driven him to Vézelay. He had returned only a few minutes before us.

"A nice location," he said, "but it has no hospital of its own. Dr. Benard tells me his hospital services a considerable area."

We were all, I think, somewhat put to it for an appropriate comment.

"Is Dr. Benard the name of your friend?" was Cornelia's.

"That's right," Sam told us, "and I've invited him and Mrs. Benard to dinner tonight. They'll be here at eight o'clock."

16

THERE were rumblings of mutiny in the women's quarters below stairs as we dressed for the unexpected dinner party. Margalo was the most recalcitrant.

"I'm not going to sit alone at the foot of the table," she declared, "listening to the rest of you jabbering French. You know it makes me nervous to hear the language. I shouldn't be surprised," she added reflectively, "if it drove me screaming mad and Dr. Sam would have to take me to the damned hospital where he picked up this doctor. I shall go to bed now and stay there. That will make things easier for everybody."

She closed her door with a firmness that was close to slamming.

Due to the proximity to one another of the cabins and the flimsiness of the partitions between them, the gesture was ineffective. From our separate rooms we talked to her and she heard us. Emily asked her to picture how crowded her isolation corner would be, since the Charles Kimbroughs had made it clear at the beginning of the trip that if anyone was in hearing distance neither of them would say aloud a French word. Sophy said she thought Margalo's absence would hurt Sam's feelings and this brought a protest from Cornelia.

"I don't want Margalo to stay below," she said, "but I doubt it would cross Sam's mind it was because she did not want to be at his party. He'd only feel sorry for her at missing the treat he was providing."

Margalo spoke but she did not open her door.

"Why didn't he ask us first if we'd consider it a treat and then ask them?"

"The idea would never remotely have crossed his mind," was Sophy's answer. "He's tolerant about our enjoyment of churches and views. I'm sure he takes it for granted we'd share his enthusiasm for people he finds interesting."

"Well, somebody should have told him," Margalo called. "When I think of the taboos we've put on others—poor Emily and Brother, for instance! I might tell him myself." Hearing that, we knew she would be at the dinner table.

The accusation was valid but, I reminded her, the other restrictions had been imposed after the occasions had overtaxed our endurance. At lunch a few days earlier yogurt had been served and Emily, seeing it, had embarked on a rhapsody we had pronounced revolting. There was nothing in the world so beneficial as yogurt, she had told us, for the colon. And she had enumerated in detail and with gusto its specific benefits. At every cry of protest from the rest of us who up to that moment had been enjoying the meal, she had turned to Sam, enlisting his corroboration. We did not wish to hear any corroboration, we had told her, nor any further exposition from her, and the rule had been passed unanimously by nine people, Sam abstaining, that Emily was not to mention the word "colon" again.

Brother had been the victim of two enforcements. He was not to use again the word *"formidable,"* pronounced in the French manner nor sing again a particular song. It was not a dirty song, there was nothing the matter with it, but Brother had sung it unexpectedly, frequently and loudly. He had learned it at about the age of twelve. It had to do with some-one riding into Granada with clanking of spur and steel. And the parts of it he did not remember he had filled in with shouts of "Olé! Olé!" On others in his environment, reading or writing, these cries had had a jumpy effect.

An injunction on Neill had not been so imperative. We had only told him it was a waste of breath to tell us what a sweet lady was the proprietress of whatever café he had visited in whatever village he had explored on his solitary prome-nades. Others of us had dropped in for a cup of coffee at the same cafés and had reported the "belle" Neill had de-scribed had been in their eyes either a blowsy, brassy har-ridan or a mumbling crone. But they had told Neill about their relatives in the United States, shown him family pictures and sent him away with a little nosegay of dismal flowers. He always came back to us with a new story, having left behind, I am sure, a contribution to the hoped-for trip one day to those relatives in America.

The finger of reproof and denial had been pointed at me because I was a sissy in a car. Since before starting I invaria-bly asked whoever was driving to go slowly, and on the route asserted to the driver he was not driving slowly, I would not be allowed in the company of those who went to fetch our Microbus. Observing a modicum of justice, they could not keep me out of the Microbus, they admitted, since I had provided it, but they would maintain their right of way in taxis necessary to retrieve it.

Remembering aloud with us these disciplines, Margalo ended her immolation and went upstairs with Sophy, Cornelia, Emily and me. Frances, quartered with Albert at the other end of the barge, knew nothing of the crisis successfully passed. She was already in the saloon when we came up the steps.

"This is going to be hell for you and me, isn't it," she inquired of Margalo, "with French going on all around us? At this moment I'd like to be somewhere else."

Margalo, with an abrupt turnabout on one heel, faced the steps again but we were a solid flank behind her. She smiled winsomely at us.

"Dear friends," she said, "I hate you venomously."

We smiled back at her, holding our ground.

There were sounds of footsteps and voices on the deck outside and on the instant two guests came through the doorway ushered in by Sam. Margalo at the head of the stairs was the first person they saw and Sam was pleased.

"How charming of you," he said, "to be waiting for us. Let me introduce you to my new friends, Mrs. Benard and Dr. Benard."

Margalo's place among the great ones in the theatre has not been reached by accident. Spreading charm, grace and warmth like perfume sprayed from an atomizer, she shook hands with the guests, smiled at Sam and waved them toward Frances and the comfortable chairs. Over her shoulder the look she turned on us would have frightened little children. We left our positions hurriedly and moved forward to be introduced. Margalo accepted her defeat, after a fashion. She did not go below. She selected, with care, a seat not far enough away to seem rude, just a distance that would put her out of the range of conversation but give her an unobstructed view. The smile never left her face; neither did a steely brightness in her eyes that had a mesmeric quality. Meeting it, in spite of determined efforts not to look in that direction, I quailed.

The seating at dinner was in the arrangement we had predicted. The General took charge of it. She also surreptitiously ordered an extra bottle of wine, thinking, correctly, an additional source of strength would be helpful.

For the rest, the dinner was not in the least as we had anticipated. Those who spoke French sat on either side of and directly across from the guests, but they had neither the need nor opportunity for much conversation. Sam was the speaker of the evening. Brimming with geniality and pride in his contribution to the voyage, he proposed toasts, made speeches. A few times his high spirits were lowered, but only momentarily. This happened when a member of the French-speaking chorus tried to interpose, in the language the Benards spoke, a translation of what Sam was saying. His outpouring was as extraordinary a combination of syllables and words as I am confident any American or French citizen has ever heard. When, prompted by desperation, these interruptions occurred, Sam would pause briefly in exasperated astonishment, then, with arm outstretched, palm upward in the gesture King Canute might have employed, would roar a command.

"Silence!" he would thunder, pronouncing it "Seelawnce."

At each of these interruptions, Margalo would half rise from her chair, directing her glass toward the one who had been cut short in his conversational effort.

"Seelawnce" was one of the few words the Benards understood. The spirit of hospitality, however, had no need of translation and they responded to it. Dr. Benard made a speech, only one and short, but appropriate. Madame Benard repeated to her neighbors how agreeable the affair was.

When the guests left at the end of the evening, Sam accompanied them along the towpath where they had parked their

car. His voice floated back to us with scarcely a pause for words or perhaps a reply from Dr. or Mrs. Benard.

In the women's dormitory below, conversation was resumed almost where it had left off when Margalo's revolt had begun. She was mollified now because, she said, we had looked as pained hearing Sam's French as she felt hearing the language at all.

Not all the time, each of us insisted; slightly hysterical through part of it, pleased that Sam was enjoying himself so thoroughly, and pained only when he used actual French words because they were invariably wrong in the context to which he applied them. He was at his best, I maintained, when he spoke in a sort of pig-Latin version of the language, obviously his own invention.

"Any of it was better than the inanities I was mouthing," Cornelia said, "and yours were no better," she added to me.

I accepted this, and for Margalo's benefit and our own relish, Cornelia and I recapitulated in English, to the best of our memory, the spritely conversation each of us had held. From the time of our student days in Paris, Cornelia and I have taken a childish and slightly idiotic pleasure in literal translations.

Cornelia began: "Ah, madame, what a grand pleasure we are taking in your so beautiful city, is it not?"

To which Madame Benard replied: "Ah, madame, but how it is genteel of your part to tell me this."

Cornelia: "But not at all, madame, I assure you, it is the verity that I speak."

"You pass very much of time in France, do you not?"

"As much as possible, is it not? It is that I love very much your country. Do you pass all the summer here?"

"Ah no, madame, it is that later we go to the Middle. Do you know the Middle?"

"Alas, no. I do not know the Middle."

I broke in. Now it was my turn to continue this brilliant repartee. "Cornelia has now turned to Dr. Benard with her witty sallies. I've just finished mine with him that consisted of a good many 'ahs' and 'is it nots' and 'is it that it is' and out of this my store of knowledge has been increased by learning that the Benards have two sons, that one is engaged in the automobile business—trucks, to be exact, is it not?"

"You said something about flowers and birds," Emily announced proudly. "I understood that."

"It was short lived," I told them. "I backed out as fast as possible. I only began it because Sam had said the doctor was a gardener and an ornithologist. After I'd asked him if he grew roses, I was finished."

Margalo was eying Sophy speculatively.

"May I ask," she inquired, "why, at one point, you scratched the doctor's stomach?"

The rest of us had not seen this and were interested too.

Sophy looked a little uncomfortable.

"It seemed appropriate at the time," she said, "but looking back on it I'm not sure it was. The doctor was saying what a high rate of heart cases the United States had. I don't know why I took exception to this but I retaliated by saying it was well known the French had bad livers. Then I wasn't sure I'd used the right word for it so I poked him there to make sure he understood."

Taking one thing with another, Emily observed, it did not seem to her that the Benards had had the most stimulating or even agreeable evening of their lives.

Sophy was immediately distressed.

"I wouldn't for the world have Sam feel disappointed," she said. "Since I've known him I've never seen him so excited and so pleased. He wanted it to be a big success. If the Benards have let him down, made him feel it was a flop, we'll have to do something to make up for it."

We had been moving in and out of our cabins, sitting on one another's beds. Sophy got up suddenly from hers.

"I think I'll just have a look upstairs. If Sam has come back I'll sound him out and maybe talk to him a little while so he won't feel too depressed."

There was not much conversation after she had left; each in her own room finishing undressing. I was just getting into bed when I heard Sophy's voice in the corridor call softly, "Whooo-whoo."

Each door opened.

"I have news for you," Sophy told us. "Sam says the Benards had such a glorious evening they are going to spend Monday on the barge with us—Monday—all day."

17

AT the post office in Auxerre the following morning, Friday, I was told I could send a telegram or a cable. I had no need at the time for these services; I had not requested either of them; I had requested stamps. I could not buy stamps. Asked the reason, the clerk with condescension and lifted eyebrows answered, "Because, as everyone knows, yesterday was Ascension Day. Therefore, certainly, stamps cannot be purchased until Monday."

It seemed to me a remarkably long time for an Ascension but I left the post office without commenting on it and set out on a shopping tour with a particular purchase in mind.

In a department store I found Sophy with the same objective and a bewildered salesman. We wanted to buy for our own use blouses such as those many French workmen wear.

Actually, they are jackets that button from top to bottom, have deep side pockets and are made of a heavy coarse cotton, almost like canvas. I had seen them appropriately worn but had thought they would be equally suitable and smart on the beach over a bathing suit, or over country clothes. I had had no idea the same thought had occurred to Sophy.

From the expression of unhappy incredulity on his face, I had the impression the salesman who had offered his services considered the idea untenable. With both hands he was endeavoring to shoo Sophy from his department, repeating querulously his merchandise was for the messieurs. Sophy, doggedly holding her ground, was matching his repeated protest with "I know that." The salesman, hearing I wished the same outlandish purchase, stopped shooing, wrung his hands, looked about wildly, obviously hoping he could catch sight of someone who would bring help or rescue him. Finally, with a shrug, he led the way resolutely to the racks where the merchandise was displayed. Turning back to us he asked hopefully if perhaps these were for our husbands. The question and the hope died as he looked at us appraisingly. With embarrassment and some distress he assured us of course we were not the wives of workingmen, and on the instant of his stammering confusion was struck so forcibly with a solution he slapped his forehead, smiling radiantly.

"But certainly," he said, "there is no question. It is very clear. You are Americans. It is I who am an imbecile."

There was no mistaking upon whom his previous conviction of imbecility had been placed, nor that the term itself was synonymous with being an American. He continued to smile and shake his head tolerantly while each of us tried on for size the jackets he offered. The tolerance leapt into cordiality when we each bought one in dark blue and one in the natural color, ecru. The look of uneasiness returned when Sophy asked if he thought washing the coats many times would reduce the blue to the faded look of the coats we had seen on workmen and liked very much. He shrugged away his misgivings as he assured us sententiously the coats would undoubtedly conform to the shade we preferred and give us increasing and long pleasure in them.

Had he remained in the doorway a little after his farewell wave, he would have seen me make another purchase. If he told in the café that evening his personal experience that day and what he had seen with his own eyes, I wonder what judgment on Americans was unanimously passed. Better, I have decided, not to think about that.

There was to me nothing irrational about purchasing three dresses at the outdoor market down the street. Two were cotton and one a silk, each in a print that in design and color I thought smarter than any I had seen in New York. They did happen to be hung from the roof of a stall whose neighbors displayed meat, vegetables, flowers, fish; a generous range of commodities.

A market stall does not include a fitting room, so I tried on the dresses in the street, over what I was wearing. When I pulled the first one over my head Sophy was the only bystander. The moment it was in place and I could look about again, I discovered I was now surrounded by a small group of men and women. They were the proprietors of nearby booths, they told me, and invited me to pay them a visit. There was no pressure of salesmanship in the invitation; it was a gesture of politeness. They had come in the spirit of camaraderie to watch me and to offer encouragement and advice. They were not reticent about either and they did not speak in whispers. From her place behind the counter in the booth, my saleslady had to exercise considerable force to make her voice heard, but she made it. As she extended one dress after another for my inspection, she called my attention to its fabric, pattern, colors, line. Each of these virtues was echoed by the members of the involuntary chorus. This had so increased in size that by the arrival of the fourth or fifth model for my approval I had been eased from a position directly across the counter from her to a stance a good ten feet away. To reach me, the dress had to be passed hand over hand, allowing time for fingering and appraisal by each one in passing. There were mixed judgments about the ones I discarded and strident differences of opinion within the group itself; but I was given unanimous approval for the ones I selected, and before the chorus disbanded I had shaken hands with and been congratulated by each member. Somewhat to her bewilderment, Sophy was included in their felicitations.

The dresses cost the equivalent of three dollars each. I have not regretted the expenditure.

Before leaving the barge that morning on our separate errands, we had set a time and place for lunch, preliminary to visiting a vineyard at Chablis. Emily, Brother, Neill, Sam, Romney, Sophy and I were to gather at twelve-thirty at a restaurant called Maxime's. Margalo and Romney had discovered it while we were in Vézelay and assured us it was both excellent and easy to find since it faced the river, not far from the bridge and the place where the *Palinurus* was moored, though she would no longer be there at lunchtime. She would have left with the Hacketts, Cornelia and Margalo remaining on board.

Learning the voyage that day would retrace a considerable portion of the waterway we had followed to reach Auxerre, Frances and Albert chose to stay on board. Their route had been by car; now they would see it from the water. Cornelia had a "raspy" throat, she said, and thought it wise to humor it. Margalo decided the expedition proposed would involve more tramping about than she favored.

The expedition was the Captain's suggestion. He had a

friend who owned a winery in Chablis. If we motored there, his friend M. Simonec would take us through his plant, and to the vineyards.

In the late afternoon, the barge would reach Brienon-sur-Armançon. We would come aboard there, and on our way from Chablis find a number of interesting places to see. It was a lovely prospect, we agreed. Richard, I think, was pleased by our enthusiastic acceptance.

The restaurant Maxime's was as easy to find as Margalo and Romney had promised and I thought even better both in appearance and food than they had described. Two chefs stood behind a counter that stretched almost the full length of the back wall. Tables were arranged on either side and in front of it. On the counter was an enticing display of foods, from lobster and other seafoods through fresh asparagus to strawberries and other fruits. The chefs cooked meats on grills in full view of the customers.

Sophy and I with our bundles were the last comers; the others had already ordered apéritifs. The General shook her head reprovingly as she ordered one.

"I suggest," she began, but with something more authoritative in her voice than suggestion, "we order no wine with lunch. Jennifer told me the day the crew was invited to Chablis they all came back in rather poor shape because of the amount of wine they'd tasted. I'm not saying this would happen to us but I do think wine now could spoil our taste and capacity for what we're going to have later."

Emily, Romney, Sam and I accepted meekly this suggestion; Neill and Brother, as if it had not been made in their hearing, shared a bottle of Pouilly Fuissé.

The way to Chablis took us over beautiful winding roads except for a brief passage along one of the big arteries. Because of its charm we were tempted to stop in the village of Chablis but agreed to postpone it until we had visited M.

Simonec, since he was probably waiting for us.

He was standing in the doorway of the winery of Simonec-le-Frebvre. A young man, short, slight, with an open smiling face, he wore a dark blue corduroy Norfolk jacket and trousers stuffed into high rubber boots. As he led the way into his plant, he began an explanation of all the processes that go into the making of wine, from growing the grapes to corking the bottles. Within fifteen minutes I felt as giddy, because of the knowledge I was absorbing, as if I had spent the time quaffing, which I had not. These are among the things I learned, and what I remember.

The finest dry white wines come from Burgundy. That of Chablis is known as a "crisp flinty-dry wine." Any Chablis that carries "Grand Cru" or "Premier Cru" has to come, by law, from one of the top seventeen vineyards of the region. When I asked M. Simonec the meaning of the word *cru* he engaged me in a kind of vocal waltz, he insisting the word could only be applied to a *premier* or a *grand,* I assuring him I realized this, but did not know what *cru* itself was. We left off a little out of breath and nothing resolved. It was only when I could put my hands on a dictionary I learned that the basic meaning of "cru" is "growth"; there is a phrase—a French phrase—to drink wine of one's own growth. Another phrase, *fruits* of a *bon cru,* means fruits of good soil. However, idiomatically, *cru* seems now to be used only as a designation of wine from the best or top vineyard.

That is the nearest I can come to a specific definition. I am still waltzing mentally. I do not know how a law can determine what one of the top seventeen vineyards of the region can qualify as the producer of the *grand* or the *premier.* I did not ask M. Simonec to explain this; I had not the endurance; furthermore, my friends were obviously growing impatient at my holding up the tour.

From the rooms where the corking and the bottling were

done, we moved into the caves. They had been built in 1840 by his forebears, M. Simonec told us, adding, "The soil here is too fluvial to have natural caves."

M. Simonec, I think, is not unhappy that the fluvial soil of his neighborhood does not produce caves, since that small area around the little town does produce all the Chablis in the world. There are about 250 property owners, he said; some of their vineyards are quite small. Three wineries receive and distribute their produce. Had anyone asked me to define a winery, I would have said it was a place where wine was made. There was no reason that day for me, unsolicited, to give my definition, but since it is almost impossible for me to keep my thoughts to myself, I did give it, to my immediate regret. M. Simonec's jolly face sobered. The tone of his voice, when he corrected me, I have heard myself use, addressing a six-year-old grandchild.

"The vineyard owners," he explained, enunciating carefully, "make their *own* wine in large casks. The wineries *buy* it. Experts taste it and pay according to the excellence of that year's crop of grapes. The function of the winery is to care for the wine properly, age it, bottle it and, finally, merchandise it."

I was thankful to God and Emily when she diverted my teacher by asking how long a wine should age. M. Simonec was shocked.

"How can you ask how long a wine should age?" he demanded rhetorically and with some vehemence.

I patted Emily's arm for comfort. I knew how she felt.

"Wine is a living thing," he continued. "You cannot make a rule. Wine is like people. Some are at their peak in youth, others do not ripen to their full potential until a middle or even an old age. For example, we have wines here," he made a sweeping gesture, "that become better and better after fifteen years. We have others whose whole life," he shrugged his shoulders, "is perhaps two years."

He moved on. We followed, Emily dropping to the rear. When he had led us through a low arched doorway and stopped beside a rack of bottles he was his jolly young self again.

"This," he said, patting one of them affectionately, "is our champagne. But, of course, we cannot call it that." He raised a hand palm outward toward Emily, then to me, forestalling any questions, I suppose.

"No," he said, "of course only the district of Champagne has the exclusive right, the patent, you might say, by law to the use of that word."

Here was the law again, I thought, functioning in a province I would have supposed outside laws. However, I fooled M. Simonec. I did not ask a question.

He looked at me inquiringly and I smiled back at him. It may have been my imagination that he seemed a little disappointed when he resumed his explanation.

"Champagne," he said, "is a sparkling white Burgundy. We call ours 'Bourgogne Mousseux.'" He shook his head regretfully. "Unfortunately," he added, "in general our Mousseux wines do not ship well."

Unprovoked by me or Emily he went into a waltz again, rendering me as giddy as if I had participated. "These wines," I think he said, "have red flesh but produce white juice. Other wines come from red grapes that give red juice, but there are also white grapes that give white juice."

He waited a moment; I made no comment. Emily beamed at him as if she knew what he was talking about. M. Simonec went on to simpler matters, the bottles.

In the production of champagnes, he said, the bottles must be given a quarter turn every day. Each hand holding the neck of a bottle in its rack, he demonstrated. There was a machine, he said, that could do this, but he preferred to have them turned by hand. With a wry smile at such absurdity, he told us this process was particularly for the benefit of Americans, who insisted on a clear wine without trace of sediment. No French person, he gave us his assurance, would dream of applying the presence or absence of sediment as a test of the quality of a wine.

This was when Sophy interrupted, with a startled exclamation. Less politely and more accurately, I would say, with a snort. In a conversation on the subject among wine experts, Sophy can acquit herself commendably. She has a discriminating palate, developed and sharpened by education. She prides herself, justifiably, on her knowledge. This reflection on American taste, and especially characterizing one manifestation of it as foolish, was not to her liking.

"I," she began, stressing the pronoun, "would not consider wine showing sediment to be of the same quality as wine without it."

M. Simonec nodded. "I know," he agreed, "that is the American way."

Sophy's face reddened; her cheeks blew out. She did not speak.

When we were shown how, in the bottle process, a series of corks was used until, after all the sediment had risen to the top, the final sealing one was applied, Sophy, somewhat ostentatiously I thought, looked in the opposite direction.

Certainly I have seen bottles of wine in racks before, but until I saw them that day in such quantity I had not realized the reason the bottom is a hollowed-out depression is to allow more bottles to be stored in less space. The neck of one set into the depression of the one ahead also holds them securely in place, preventing a bottle landslide. The picture this arrangement incongruously brought to my mind was a procession of elephants; the tail of one held by the trunk of the next in line.

A winery, I learned, is not so meticulous about cleaning bottles as about storing, corking and turning them. They are handled carefully to avoid breakage because bottles are very expensive, M. Simonec said, and rapidly increasing in price. Wine merchants, at least in the district, are meticulous about returning any empty bottles they may have, though there is no rebate on them. However, bottles old and new are not sterilized: they are washed, that is all. I choose to believe their ultimate alcoholic content sterilizes them.

On the other hand, we learned the vats or casks when emptied are thoroughly cleaned, and of all things, with sulphur. I put my foot in the middle of M. Simonec's explanation by asking why they did not use water.

M. Simonec was aghast. "Water," he explained, "would soak into the wood, never dry, and ruin the flavor."

The ignorant will have to learn from someone else why a sulphur solution, of all things, does not affect the flavor. I did not ask. I put my face down over the opening in a cask that was being cleaned and very nearly stretched my length on the floor of the cave. It took half an hour for my eyes to stop watering; nevertheless, I repeat, the flavor of wine is not affected.

We left the winery to walk to the nearest of the vineyards, about a quarter of a mile away along a dirt road. When I was a child in Muncie, Indiana, we had a grape arbor with a swing under it. The swing had two seats facing each other with a platform between. If you stood on the platform, by shifting your weight from one foot to the other, you could ride the swing alone and, at the same time as you moved, pick grapes from overhead—a little like catching the brass ring on the merry-go-round. The smell was delicious and so was the speckled shade the arbor made.

There was no smell nor shade from these grapevines, and you could not have swung your hand underneath one.

Wretched, stunted little things, I would have called them. The ones we saw were about eight inches high but they had far more tender, loving care than was given our grapes in Muncie. There were smudge pots along each row and these had been burning all the night before because the weather had been cool. Since they stretched almost out of sight, this represented considerable work; each of these had been set out and put into operation by hand. M. Simonec pointed out a machine on the top of the hill nearby. Its purpose, he said, was to blow warm air over a wide area. At his request, we admired it.

He lost me once more when he talked about the "eyes" of each plant or shoot. "There must be twenty," I think, he said, and he pointed them out to us.

I was unable to see anything that looked like an eye. I do not know if the number twenty is correct and I have not the slightest idea of the purpose of one or twenty "eyes." At that one moment in my life, I was disinclined to ask a question.

18

A Volkswagen Microbus is a lovely vehicle with a beautiful nature, even-tempered and accommodating. It does not fume about climbing hills nor sputter over a load of eleven passengers and considerable luggage. When not in motion, however, it is not my first choice of places in which to sit three hours during a rainstorm.

We explored the town of Chablis after leaving the vineyards. We walked on the promenade du Pâtis along the Serein River. It is bordered by beautiful and very old trees. We trudged into breathless exhaustion, up and around narrow winding streets, to find the Eglise of St. Martin. M. Simonec had urged this visit if only to see the *fers à chevaux,* he said, and refused smilingly to explain how and why we would find horseshoes in a church. They were not in the church; they covered the outer side of the broad Romanesque entrance doors. Together with the church itself, the doors date from the thirteenth century. So do the "strap hinges" and the horseshoes nailed there by pilgrims as votive offerings to St. Martin. The legend is that one of these offerings was placed by Joan of Arc.

From the church we returned to the car and settled in with sighs of contented relief, stretching legs made weary and aching by our pilgrimage through caves, vineyard and town.

The rain began and the temperature dropped as we left Chablis. In Auxerre we had drunk apéritifs at tables outside the café where we lunched and taken off sweaters because the sun was so hot. There had been no cloud in the sky to warn of rain. It must have been an undeserved guardian angel who had directed us to take our coats. We put them on now and still shivered, the car windows closed. We yearned to drive straight to our dear mother barge but we were orphans in the storm. Seeing us off at Auxerre, Captain Richard had named again Brienon the place where we would meet, but he could not be sure of the time. Certainly it would be late afternoon, he had said; there was much water to cover and possibly traffic would delay them. He had suggested we dally along the way by stopping at Pontigny. Its abbey was well worth seeing and certainly we would not want to spend the entire afternoon with M. Simonec.

Heading dismally for Pontigny, the rain thumping on the roof and spattering under the wheels, we admitted to one another each of us privately had thought it unlikely we would see the famous abbey, more likely we would spend the entire afternoon with M. Simonec. Not that a tour of the cellars and vineyard would require so much time, but the wine tasting that must follow the tour should not be hurried. We would pay M. Simonec and the occasion the courtesy of a deliberate and contemplative savoring, discriminating compliments and a leisurely enjoyment of the inner warmth as it was gradually instilled. Thanks to Sophy's anticipation of this rosy future only Neill and Brother had ignored, we had been deprived at lunch of a bottle of wine.

The wine tasting for which this sacrifice had been made had occupied perhaps a minute and a half of our time. It had not taken place in M. Simonec's office nor in any room. Walking through a cellar he had stopped at one of the casks. He had brought down from a shelf above it a tiny glass for each of us and a slender glass tube. Earnestly assuring us the wine would not reach his lips, he had put one end of the tube in his mouth and inserted the other through an opening in the side of the cask. With, to me, fascinating adroitness, he had sucked into the tube an amount of wine so exact it did not reach his lips. Withdrawing then the tube, he had emptied its contents on the floor, to remove, I suppose, any surface sediment. With the same accuracy of amount he had siphoned off and emptied a tubeful for each glass. I have never drunk out of a thimble so I do not know relatively the amount of a thimbleful, but my conjecture is it would have served as a measuring cup for the contents of the tube. It had not been easy to sip because one swallow would have drained the glass. I had not needed Sophy's head shaken and lips pursed to tell me wine at such a time should be rolled on the tongue and even before that sniffed with a suitable comment about its bouquet. I knew the things I should do and I had meant to do them and had in fact sniffed and declared the aroma exquisite, though actually I had smelled nothing whatever; but my first sip had been a swallow and one swallow had drained the glass. I had immediately put my hand around it and pretended to continue sipping. It had been a disconcerting experience and thoroughly unsatisfactory in content and effect.

Thinking about this in the chill of the Microbus, I wondered uneasily if Emily's and my revealed ignorance had

reduced M. Simonec's hospitality. If we had kept quiet then we might feel warmer now.

Conversation lagged; the dampness outside had got through to us. Gradually, however, and a little reluctantly we began to take note of the landscape around us and point it out to one another. It was not like any we had seen before. The vistas were as wide as those on the way to Vézelay but the terrain was not so hilly. This was the first landscape we had seen in the rain. In sunlight of course colors had been sharply defined one against another, the mustard always slashing through fields in themselves of different shades of green. Now they were blended to a misty gray.

"Well," Emily said abruptly, "those painters never should have been called Impressionists. That gives people like me a wrong impression. They were realists. They painted exactly what they saw. Look at it." Sophy at the wheel, of course, interrupted.

"We should be coming near Pontigny," she said. "Have you the guidebook, Neill?" A foolish question, I pointed out, because just as Sophy always took the wheel Neill always took the guidebooks.

Neill volunteered to share the information he was acquiring and read aloud.

"Pontigny, on the edge of the river Serein, is celebrated for its former abbey founded in 1114. The abbey church is a fine example of Cistercian art. During the Middle Ages Pontigny served as refuge for bishops from England. Three Archbishops of Canterbury successively found asylum there. Thomas à Becket having incurred the anger of King Henry II of England came to Pontigny in 1164."

He was still reading when Sophy broke in. "This must be Pontigny."

Had she not been on the alert, we might easily have gone through the village, it is so tiny. Actually we were on its rim when she identified the place. We could not have passed without noticing a little farther on, a long avenue bordered with old trees. Our suggestion this must be the way to the church was as superfluous as the question had been of who had the guidebook. Sophy had already turned into it. Three-quarters of the way down, she stopped the car at an arched gateway on our left. We looked through into a beautiful garden enclosed in a border of yews easily eight feel tall and in topiary. Neill urged us unnecessarily to share his pleasure in the sight. The trees he said were very old. The building beyond we knew from the guidebook was a restored abbey and presently occupied by the Mission de France.

We did not leave the car until we had reached the church itself, where there was parking space. We entered in the customary way by a small side door, pushed open an inner one and stood literally stunned at the length of the magnificent aisle we faced. Under a succession of Romanesque arches it stretched away before us. The façade of the church had given no indication of the size of the interior. If Neill had read aloud its dimensions I was not listening, since the door of my mind automatically closes at the approach of figures. Later, going back to the guidebook myself, I read, skipping the actual number of feet, that the church is almost as large as Notre Dame. Though I respond happily to the flamboyant in architecture I was deeply moved by its absence here. I think the others felt, too, the solemnity of its austerity, because, though we had not chattered in any church, here we walked about on tiptoe, not exchanging so much as a whisper until we had come outside again when Brother said in a small voice, "Any other suggestion Richard makes of what to see I'll be glad to follow."

Perhaps when we left we were still a little cowed by the disciplined severity we had just seen, because we talked very little. Aware of our silence I realized how different the effect of other churches had been. Coming away from richness in design and color we had exploded into animated appreciation of what we had just seen, our spirits uplifted, but not subdued. I was about to share with Romney this train of thought, asking him what effect he thought a church itself had on its congregation, when I remembered he did not like any churches, therefore it was not a particular one that had quenched his usual loquacity. He must have received a telepathic communication because he spoke.

"It's raining harder than ever," he said, "very depressing." That opinion was evidently unanimously though tacitly endorsed, because there was no other remark from anyone.

Brienon did not change our outlook. We found it unprepossessing and dismal. We reached it about half past five. The streets were deserted, the rain almost torrential. We drove around the village looking out with a lackluster eye; this was probably why we did not see the medieval community laundromat Richard told us about the next day. Under a roof, a running stream, he said, of crystal clear and icy water runs through a long stone basin with a broad rim on which the washing can be laid flat and scrubbed. Like any woman's clubhouse, he had added, it was usually crowded.

We did see the bridge! In a village that size it was not difficult to find. The bridge was our appointed trysting place but it also marked another point in our journey. We looked down on a water channel that was narrow, symmetrical, bordered with trees along its clean-cut banks. We had left the rivers behind; we had reached the Burgundy Canal.

From the bridge we saw on one side a wide ramp leading to a paved area ample for parking. There was a stone building behind it, perhaps a warehouse. From the other side, a narrow rutted steep path ended in woods along the bank of the canal. Without hesitation Sophy took us down this path because the view that included a bend just ahead in the waterway was more picturesque. We jolted to a stop when it was impossible to go farther. No one ventured a query about getting back to the highway. Romney, however, did pose a pertinent question. From which direction, he asked, would the *Palinurus* come? Should he strain his eyes ahead or incur a crick in the neck by watching over his shoulder?

Had there been more than two directions from which to

choose I do not know to what proportions the ensuing discussion might have swelled. I took no part in it since I know where I am only if I have gone that way before, and I recognize east and west and their neighbors only when I am looking directly into a rising or a setting sun.

With maps and arguments the others exhausted themselves and me. While they wrangled, other barges came slowly in and out of our sight. They were beautiful long sleek oil tankers, freshly painted and polished, nothing like a "Dirty British coaster . . . With a cargo of Tyne coal." Their cargo was oil, though the only evidence of it was the name of the company on the flying pennant. The *Palinurus* was not in the procession.

The rain had grown less violent and gusty, but it was steady. The temperature was dropping. Romney asked another question even more unhappily provocative than his first. Reminding us that, filling a commission from Richard, we were bringing back from Chablis fifty bottles of wine, he inquired if any of us happened to have a corkscrew. That bit of lead, taking soundings of our depression, might have marked its nadir, had Emily not wondered aloud what we would do if the *Palinurus* did not come at all. With so much traffic as we had seen coming through, she amplified, our barge might easily have been shunted aside by the big tankers and have to moor until the locks opened the next morning.

This appalling possibility had the surprising effect of rousing some members from the sodden lethargy in which we were wrapped, to an activity that seemed to me demented. Opening the door beside him Neill stepped from the front seat into the rain. Simultaneously Brother directly behind him did the same. Emily scrambled after them saying, "Where are you going? I'm coming too."

"To find a café," was Neill's answer and Brother echoed, "That was my idea."

Over our shoulders Sophy, Romney, Sam and I watched them plod up the hill behind us and, reaching the highway, turn toward the village.

"When they come back," Romney prophesied, "Neill will tell us the café is run by a charming creature who made them welcome and showed photographs of relatives in America."

Sophy nodded agreement. "And the Kimbroughs will inform us privately the café is run by a crone of eighty-odd summers without teeth or relatives, but that Neill wooed her extravagantly and she responded with extra-sized hospitality."

Both forecasts were accurate. The hospitality induced by Neill had spilled over into brandy with the coffee they had ordered, but the only thing the scouts brought back was the information that we were headed in the wrong direction, and that the narrow picturesque lane down which we had come was considerably muddier than it had been when the car had made the descent. Brother, with a mellow cheerfulness the situation did not warrant, asked Sophy if she had realized turning the car around was impossible. Sophy without cheerfulness answered she had realized it. The Café Society group climbed into the car. Sam and I simultaneously got out with the idea in mind that Sam voiced:

"If you have to back up the hill I'll stand in the highway and try to keep the place open for you."

We stood in the center of the highway not much more apart than the width of the car. We stood with arms outstretched like semaphores, and almost on the instant after assuming this position, ran to either edge for safety. Cars approaching gave unmistakable indication their drivers had no intention of paying the slightest heed to our signals, and that if we chose to be run down it was of course our own decision. We made several attempts that followed the same pattern, but at a moment when we were out of breath from our sorties and ignominious retreats the road was inexplicably empty of cars. We beckoned. The General slowly, majestically backed up the lane and into the highway. At the moment she reached it traffic reappeared as unexpectedly as it had ceased. This did not disconcert the General. While I cowered by a roadside bush, sweating at the sight, longing to cover my ears against the inevitable crunching of an inevitable impact, our imperturbable mentor not only backed into but made a slow and complete turn around on the highway. Her assumption that no one would accost or even threaten whatever plan she is executing is a quality I admire and lack.

When Sam and I joined the car she had brought it down a gentle incline to the wide parking space on the other side. It was not so picturesque as the lane had been, but it did afford ample space in which to turn around. In order to go where? Emily inquired with dismal acumen. Three more tankers passed. It was half past seven.

Simultaneously Romney and I identified far in the distance a familiar and beloved shape and we shouted it in the same breath. The others were incredulous of our farsightedness, and irritated. We were asked to keep quiet and not raise their hopes. Their fretful griping was extinguished as abruptly and simultaneously as our shout had come. Even they saw, standing on the deck of the craft we had identified for them, figures waving their arms, jumping up and down, someone twirling a scarf in the air. Our dear marines were landing.

What a reunion! We might have been returning from years of adventure in the Crusades, but after all we had been almost forty miles away. By our joy in being restored to the bosom of our mother ship, by warmth again outer and inner, by way of a glorious dinner and comforting wine, we enjoyed a foolish evening. In the course of it Sophy followed her, to Bobs and me, well-known pattern of expression. When she has

emerged from an anxiety and is in the company of understanding friends she dresses up. That evening she outdid any
previous displays of her creation I had seen. The fashion show she produced, in the style, somewhat exaggerated,
of a mannequin, included the workmen's blouses she had
purchased and my three dresses from the street fair. They
were graced by accessories I doubt will ever accompany them
again. Cornelia, not to be outdone, followed her in a seduc-
tive Oriental creation. It was some minutes before I recognized the yashmak over which she winked coquettishly had

earlier been a scarf I usually tied around my head, and that the draped partial covering below was my bathrobe.

We went to sleep to the sound of rain against the window pane, delicious and sleep provoking, not in the least, I thought drowsily, as it had sounded on the roof and sides of the car while we sat in the lane.

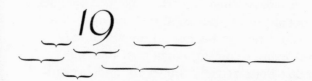

OTHER tourists who have visited St. Florentin remember the cathedral. It is starred in the guidebook. The post office is not mentioned, but it is the building Emily, Brother and I will remember and for all time associate with the town. We spent there a period of time whose minutes were not winged but fitted with the leaden shoes of a diver. Nevertheless, the visit was rewarding. When we came away, we had bought stamps.

Sometime during the night the rain had stopped. The morning was bright and after an early start we had reached St. Florentin by half past ten. Told by Richard we had a wait of two hours, we had left the barge immediately. Unlike the usual pattern, we had not scattered the minute we had quitted the barge. An unexpected sight had drawn the group together again. Sophy and I, the last to come ashore, had seen the others transfixed and magnetized. In England and Wales on another barge trip we had seen such unnatural superimposing as was rendering our friends idiotic. Trying, unsuccessfully I think, not to sound patronizing, I told them Sophy and I were not so taken aback as they because we had experienced a like phenomenon. The channel in which our boat moved was a bridge that in turn spanned a river.

Margalo's crisp comment was that to have seen a calf with two heads twice would not make the phenomenon commonplace at the second viewing. To travel on one channel of water, and, looking down, see another running beneath at right angles, would remain for her an unnatural experience no matter how many times she might pass that way.

The river that flows at right angles to, and beneath the Burgundy Canal at that point is the Armançon. The town of St. Florentin rests on terraces around a hill, like a ruffled skirt tapering to a slender waist, where the church stands high and stately. We rested too on the way to it: the hill is steep, with enough side streets to allow us to climb separate ways. The one I chose passed arched gateways set in the walls Sam, before his conversion, had disliked. Beyond the gateways were lovely gardens, cascades of wisteria against one house and over the threshold. Tall lilacs were in full bloom, also tulips, and in one I saw, for the first time on this trip, peonies. Although the upper part of the church dominates the surrounding landscape, the first view of its entirety is from the far end of a long *allée* of trees and it is superb. The Michelin guidebook says the church was begun in 1376 and completed in 1614. A brochure available at the church itself and called *Guide du Visiteur* says the church dates from the sixteenth and seventeenth centuries. It is not within my province of knowledge to endorse one and chide the other. I have only enough knowledge of periods to identify as Renaissance the costumes of Biblical characters in the stained-glass windows, and they are charming anachronisms. The colors in the glass are rich and deep and in one window unusual shades to find in stained glass, beige and brown pointed up by bright orange.

As I came out of the church I saw Cornelia and Sophy a little to one side of the entrance looking up with rapt concentration at something over their heads. When I spoke they neither answered nor turned their heads, but simultaneously pointed upwards.

"What does that look like to you?" Sophy inquired.

I gave a composition sculptured in stone my close scrutiny and considered judgment.

"An angel dancing on a pyramid of three cubes—oh, dice!"

My friends nodded.

"That's what we thought," Cornelia agreed, "but it seemed unlikely."

A pedestrian on Fifth Avenue in New York who stops a moment to look up at the sky will collect around him a sizable crowd all looking upward. The narrow winding street to the church of St. Florentin is not reminiscent of Fifth Avenue, but three people craning their necks drew a participating group though when I had come out of the church there had been no one in sight except my two friends. When we turned from our fascinated study of the piece of church sculpture we were surprised to see how much the study group had increased. Even more embarrassed than surprised we scuttled around the group muttering inanities to the people on its edge who looked at us inquiringly.

"Your church is so beautiful, we are Americans, we are admiring so much your city and it is that the church is magnificent, is it not?"

As the little crowd was dispersing and we were abashedly endeavoring to shake our skirts of it, who should come up over the top of the hill but Brother and Emily panting a little. At sight of us Brother called, "What's going on? We saw people coming this way. Is there a procession?"

"Oh, for God's sake," I answered irritably, "it's nothing on earth but an angel dancing on three dice."

They are people of determination. I could not persuade them to come away until I had shown them the quixotic adornment, surreptitiously so as not to draw an audience again. I hold against them, too, the visit to the post office. Emily was the one who wanted stamps but she would not go alone to buy them. I had in mind exploring the town in case there might be antique shops. Brother admitted to a sneaker for a jersey pullover of the sort French bicyclists wear. What we set out for were stamps. Sophy left us to explore the town. Cornelia was returning to the barge. She had had enough, she said, of everything.

The post office of St. Florentin stands on a corner where two streets converge sharply. It is not much to look at from the outside and has a dismal interior. My relatives joined a line standing in front of a grilled window with the sign "Timbres" above it. I sat down on a bench against the wall. Had I not done that because my legs were tired I might have missed two signs that gave me deep pleasure. One identified the section below it as the "Caisse Nationale de Prévoyance." By my translation this is the National Counter or Cash Room of Foresight. If I were French, I thought, I would find it reassuring to know there was a place in my local post office to which I could go when I needed foresight on a national scale. On another wall I read a framed illustrated announcement of a telegraph service. "These Illustrated Telegrams Deluxe," it read, "carry a surtax of the heart." The reproduction of this illustrated telegram deluxe included in one corner a large bouquet of flowers in staggeringly bright and assorted colors.

Have we in America, I asked myself, a surtax on the heart carried by telegram? And I answered myself no. While I was ruminating enviously on the benefits France was offering, Brother and Emily reached the head of the line and almost immediately summoned me. Emily's eyes, very brown and very large, were more than ever like a startled deer's.

"I think the man is telling us," she said when I had reached them, "I cannot send these letters and postcards airmail to America."

She indicated the pile of mail she had pushed under the window to a thin elderly stooped clerk whose eyes were not so large but as apprehensive as Emily's.

Brother was nodding agreement. "That's what I think he's saying."

I addressed myself in French to the clerk. "Is it possible, monsieur," I inquired, "that it is not possible to send these letters and postcards to the United States by airmail?"

The old gentleman spread tremulous hands palm upward and lifted his shoulders to his ears.

"Ah, madame," he said, "it is not certainly that it is not possible, it is only that I have not the proper stamps. It is therefore necessary that I make the computations among stamps of other prices to arrive at the proper number and amount, is it not?"

Certainly it was. I let him know I was with him.

"Then, madame," he continued, extending a hand toward me to make us one in understanding, "certainly you will know that this will have need of time and of work and it might be that you are pressed," the soft brown eyes were pleading pitifully, "and do not have the time for waiting and so you would take the ordinary stamps that I have do you see at my hand and if the messages are perhaps not so important?" His voice trailed up to a hopeful question.

Three heads shaken in unison convinced him there was no way out. Nevertheless, I explained. It is a failing of which I am often accused.

"You see, monsieur," I told him, "we come from the United States very far away. I have twin daughters; each is married, I have seven grandchildren. This is my brother and sister-in-law," indicating my companions. "They too have children, a son and a daughter. The son is married and they are expecting their first baby."

"Why don't you tell him you were born in Muncie, Indiana," Brother muttered, "and that I went to Yale?"

I ignored the interruption.

"So you see we do not write these letters to amuse ourselves. They are to say we are well and that everything marches, so the young mother expecting her baby can remain tranquil and that my grandchildren can have education from the postcards of the beautiful places in your country we are seeing and so everything must go quickly."

The old man sighed deeply. "It is indeed so," he conceded and drew up a high stool.

From a drawer beneath the counter he took a copybook such as children use at school. He closed the drawer and seated himself on the stool, drawing it to the counter. Stretching as far as the bars of the window would permit because I wanted to watch this undertaking, I saw him twist his legs around the rungs of the stool, a substitute I thought for a clenched fist, that would emphasize his determined saying to himself, "If this thing has got to be done let's get on with it."

From arm's reach he brought a memorandum pad and placed it beside the copybook—meticulously because he shifted it three times. This pad was an assemblage of small pieces of paper, backs of envelopes, scraps of stationery, brown pieces, undoubtedly left over from wrapping a package. They were held together by a string run through a hole that had been punched in the top of each.

From a rack in front of him the mathematician selected three pencils, but the selections were not entirely to his liking. He took a penknife from the same tray, opened it carefully and certainly slowly, placed each pencil in turn point down on the top sheet of the memorandum pad and, bending low over it to gauge exactly how far to go, sharpened the point. He arranged the pencils in a row at the top of and just beyond the copybook, eased the pad to the edge of the counter, blew delicately the graphite to the floor, waved the pad in the air, inspecting it between times, and only when it bore no trace of the recent operation performed on it, replaced it as meticulously as he had selected its position. Evidently there was no further delay that occurred to him. With a heartrending sigh he opened the copybook. It held between the pages the stamp supply, the denominations separated. I am sure the greatest number of these could not have been more than twenty. There was no index, even homemade, to show between what pages what stamps or any stamps could be found. So our lightning calculator had to turn each one in order to find and spread before him the material for his figuring.

The post office of St. Florentin will have to make a new memorandum pad. This one can never be used again. Both sides of every sheet were covered with figures; the pencils had to be resharpened.

Something, perhaps a telepathic cry for help, attracted the notice of the postmaster. Through an open door behind the counter I had seen a man with an air and position of authority, seated at a large flat desk. He rose, came without haste to the clerk, leaned forward, patted his shoulder, made an inquiry in a low tone. The clerk without looking up nodded miserably and showed the array of stamps spread before him and his calculations. The postmaster patted him again, returned to his inner sanctum and reappeared a minute later with a sheet of airmail stamps of the denominations proper for America. Evidently these were so precious he must have kept them put away in a safe.

Though pathetically grateful for his salvation, the clerk now had to start his calculations all over again, not, however, before he had returned to their proper places all the stamps he had accumulated—each denomination between two pages in the copybook. After this he dove again into figures. He was no wizard at addition but after three or four tries he reached a sum he liked or at least accepted and we did not question it.

Coming out of the building we were surprised to find it was still daylight. On our way to the barge we overtook Frances and Sophy, Frances triumphant because she had found a workman's blouse. Sophy, commissioned by Cornelia, had bought one for her. I was not happy to learn they had loitered at a number of antique shops and I did not care to hear what the others had done.

When we came on the barge Margalo and Romney were playing solitaire at separate tables; Emma was behind the bar. Nothing had changed. I wondered if this was the way it had seemed to Marco Polo returning.

As I started down the stairs to my cabin Emma called: "Richard wants me to tell everyone we now have a supply of stamps on board. You can buy them from me."

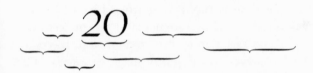

20

IN the early hours of the morning I wakened suddenly with an uneasy conviction someone was in the room. I was right. Miranda, the expectant mother cat, was sitting at the foot of my bed, looking at me with the concentration of a hypnotist, her eyes glowing in the dark. Having wakened me—and I know she had done it deliberately—she moved slowly up the bed, putting down each foot experimentally much the way I go into the ocean. Just as I, deciding on a spot that is neither too shallow nor too deep, lower myself to a swimming position, Miranda, deciding on an area immediately over my stomach, lowered herself and began to dig the bedclothes. She was unmistakably making a nest for her approaching *accouchement* but her satisfaction at finding just the right place for it was not mine. I did not wish to be pushed into a confinement along with hers. I did feel, however, her condition justified the squatter's rights she was taking. I could not evict her into a drafty corridor. I would give up my prior claim. Easing out from under her I took a pillow and from the foot of the bed a blanket.

"It's all yours," I told Miranda and left the cabin. At the opposite end of the corridor and across from Sam's, there was an unoccupied stateroom. We had stored our luggage there, but the bed was unoccupied; it was also unmade. Even with only one blanket and pillow I preferred it to rooming with Miranda. I was struggling to reach around my encumbrances in order to open the door without noise when I heard Jenny's voice in the saloon above. The cadence and accent were unlike Emma's and unmistakable, but recognition was startling because I had never heard Jenny speak so loudly. The stairway was only a few feet beyond where I was standing. I tiptoed to its foot and looked up. If I could attract the attention of that skilled animal handler I could return to my own quarters and she would cope with Miranda elsewhere. Before I could say "hist" or any other attention-getting sound, I saw feet whirl across the head of the stairs, a girl's and a man's. They were dancing. I went up a few steps—not enough for my head to show—heard singing and behind the voices a harmonica, so I knew Jacques was playing and Jenny must be dancing with David. This was more surprising than the sound of Jenny's voice. I would not have thought David could dance. To me he had seemed a solid, substantial man but heavy, and had thought it strange that Jenny, a little drop of quicksilver, had been drawn to him. David was not dancing. A voice from the vicinity called harshly; no one could have mistaken the Midlands accent.

"Will you stop that, Jenny, or will I give you a clout will drop ye?"

"Come off it, David, let her have some fun."

: *184* :

I would not have recognized Richard's voice had the others not been accounted for, and thought even David's the more likely to be the dancing feet. For all his lithe, slim body, Richard had been so serious his years had seemed doubled by the responsibility as captain and owner that hung heavy, heavy over them. He would not have astonished me more had he capered into a sailor's hornpipe for the entertainment of his passengers. The dancers passed me again. With a hand out I could have touched them. Emma was singing a French song.

"Leave be, David, leave be. Only tonight for Richard's party." That was Jenny. At the same moment Richard called, "I'm opening another bottle of wine."

Why David's answering roar did not waken every passenger I cannot imagine. I should have thought, like the foghorn it resembled, the sound would have reached the nearby village. Perhaps it seemed louder to me because the place on the stairs in which I stood made a kind of funnel, but its quality was terrifying.

"You'll pay for this, Jenny, and you don't need me to tell you. And I'll not tell you again."

The harmonica and the singing stopped abruptly. In the silence his voice sounded louder and more frightening.

The dancing feet were stilled. Perhaps Richard was going to remonstrate with David.

David shouted again, "You're coming now and I'll lock you up," then evidently to Richard: "And don't you raise your little finger to stop me or I'll knock you down."

Jenny screamed, "Don't lay hands on him, David, don't touch me either. Keep away, keep away."

Suddenly she was on the top step and by God's mercy I was not there too. Panicked I had backed down to the foot of the stairs in bewilderment and fright. I was reluctant to rouse Brother and the other men. I did not want them laid out one by one by David and certainly he sounded and looked capable of it. Should I try to appease him and perhaps shame him into mollifying his threats? Obviously he was going to give Jenny a beating and certainly I was not going to let that happen.

In her flight down the stairs I think she would have rushed past without seeing me, but I stepped in front of her with my arms out. The body was Jenny's but her face almost unrecognizable, eyes wild, feverish, her skin chalk white, her black hair that had lain so smooth and flat to her head tangled and bristling out in all directions. I closed my arms around her and she struggled to break away, still seeming to have no recognition of me. Surely David would be upon her at any moment, I thought, though I was aware of his voice no longer shouting but persistently calling her.

"Listen to me, Jenny," I urged, and pulled her, still fighting me, away from the foot of the stairs, "I won't let David hurt you. Come to my room."

She seemed not to hear me.

"He'll lock me up, he'll lock me up and I won't be closed in." Her voice shook and her body trembled. "Let me go."

There was nowhere she could go without encountering David unless I could persuade her to hide in my cabin. The only way to the quarters for the crew was by a stairway from the stern just back of the galley. To reach it she would have had to go up our stairs again into the saloon, cross its length to reach her own area. I said over and over I would not let David hurt her. She must stay with me. She was not listening or if she heard did not understand. It suddenly occurred to me if I mentioned the cat I might get through to her. I had completely forgotten Miranda and the reason I was there.

"Listen, Jenny," I said and shook her a little, "Miranda is having kittens, Miranda, Miranda, Miranda."

For the first time Jenny's eyes focused on me.

"Miranda? Miranda?" she echoed and recognized the name and me simultaneously. "Where is she? Is anything the matter?"

"In my cabin." I said the words slowly, "She is having her kittens."

Jenny pushed me aside as if I had weighed ninety pounds and she one hundred and forty and ran down the corridor. Before I could reach it she was out again, Miranda in her arms. She flashed past me up the stairs.

"I'm coming, David," I heard her call. "The cat's going to birth."

When I reached my room I was sick in my washbasin, and when I let myself fall on the bed I was trembling so I could not crawl under the covers. The blanket and pillow were still at the foot of the stairs where I had dropped them when Jenny plunged down, but I had not strength enough to retrieve them. I had had to lean against the wall twice to steady myself before I could reach the cabin. Of course I did not sleep. I told myself what a coward I was, and alternately what a fool, not to trust Richard's control of his boat and crew. I kept seeing Jenny's face, eyes staring, hair disheveled. Some time after daylight I made myself go back to the end of the corridor, up the stairs, across the saloon to the crew's stairway. I listened there a minute or two, but there was not a sound from below, and then I pelted back the way I had come, snatching up my blanket and pillow on the way; in my bed again I finally dropped off to sleep.

When I came up for breakfast next morning several of the others were ahead of me. Emma was pouring coffee; Jacques had just arrived from the village with fresh bread and croissants. They both looked fresh and serene. Jacques had been whistling until he came into the saloon. Sometimes Richard would go through the room to say good morning on his way to forward deck to cast off. David never came inside.

We only saw him up at his post in the stern when we went on deck. Sometimes a shadow falling from one window and then the next across the tables where we ate would mean Jenny was running along on her way to do up our rooms. No shadow danced past us that morning, Richard did not come through, but I could not bring myself to ask Emma about Jenny. Anything I asked would acknowledge I knew something of the night before.

By nine o'clock everyone was settled on the deck. The day was bright and warm, and the countryside we glided by, green and, for all our slow, measured pace, varied. Settled is an inaccurate term to apply to the group. Though Romney dozed and Margalo lying in her chair watched the passing scene with a smile of blissful somnolence, Sophy and Brother took pictures on either side. Out from the bow, in from the bow, climbing on whatever foothold would give a desired height, steadying each other, Emily hovering around them offering suggestions that evoked no audible nor visible response. Frances read, interrupting herself frequently to bring from her coat pocket, study and then replace, her compass. Neill sketched, coaxed by the beauty of the day from the table in the saloon covered with guidebooks and maps that had become his office. Albert and Sam inched a passage along the outside walk, followed by apprehensive though soft cries from Frances to call on David at the wheel. I was the most unsettled member. Several times I went inside, saying I wanted another book, as if anyone cared. The beds in the cabins were made, the doors were open as I went down the corridor, but Jenny was not in sight. My room had not the scrubbed look she usually left. Upstairs in the little kitchen—nautical vocabulary embarrasses me—Jacques was preparing lunch. I could hear him whistling but when I called Emma's name he heard me and answered that she was in her own room; he would fetch her if I wanted something. I told him

quickly it was not in the least important; I would see her at
lunchtime. With a deep breath before I lost courage, I asked
if he had seen Jenny. I thought there was a slight pause before he answered but I was standing in the middle of the
saloon and could not see him. His reply was laconic.

"Oh, she's about," he said in French, "sometimes here,
sometimes there, but just now she too is in her room. You do
not need her?"

"Not at all, not at all," I assured him redundantly and
went out once more onto the deck.

While Emma was putting together the small tables and
setting them for lunch I wanted to speak to her, but the
others had followed me in from the deck and were waiting at
the bar for her to take over there.

We moored early that afternoon, and I was the first one off
the barge. Without waiting for anyone I walked away
quickly. Someone, I think it was Sophy, called me but I pretended not to hear. During the morning she had commented
on my restlessness at some moment when she and Brother
were scrambling about with their cameras. I do not know
why I was reluctant to share my experience of the night before, except perhaps I did not want any of the others to become uneasy with a suspicion that all was not well below deck
and that another outbreak might occur. On my two-hour
walk I did not meet anyone from the barge. When I returned
none of the group was aboard. Jenny was in my cabin. Except
that she was pale and with dark circles under her eyes, she
was the Jenny I knew. Her black hair was smooth and like a
cap close to her head, her eyes were bright and she was
smiling.

"I was waiting for you," she said. "I think I saw you last
night, didn't I?"

"Yes, you did," I told her miserably and put my arm
around her. "Are you all right, dear? Nothing happened to

you? I tried to keep you with me but you wouldn't stay. Are you all right?" I repeated. And then because I could not help asking what had haunted me all day I blurted, "Did David hurt you?"

She stared at me in astonishment, her eyes wide, her mouth open a little.

"David hurt me? Why, David couldn't hurt anybody or anything. He's the kindest man you'll ever see."

I am sure my look of astonishment equaled hers. She took my arm from around her shoulder, patted it, indicating the bed.

"Sit down," she said, "do. I've come to tell you about it," and sat down beside me.

"I have the petit mal. It's much better now and mostly because of David. I had to stop school because of it but it got better. Doctors know a lot more about it now. Still, when I had a job as kennel maid in Canada I told the lady, of course, about it and any other job I've had. David knew but he wouldn't give up the idea of marrying me. He said he would take care of me and I was going to be well and that's what's happened almost, and it's all because he sees to it I don't get excited. The life on the barge is just right and, of course, David wouldn't be happy anywhere else. But once in a while, it doesn't happen often any more, I want excitement so bad I can't stand it and David knows it and he knows I'll pay for it. So last night we went ashore. It was really for Richard. He takes his job and the responsibility so hard he was all tied up in knots and I decided he had to get relaxed. Of course he knows all about my trouble but we got him to drink some wine so he forgot about it. Well of course when I get some wine I forget about it too and I expect I get pretty wild. I want to sing and dance and never stop, but David knows I have to stop."

She laughed as unselfconsciously and gleefully as a mischievous child. "But I won't heed him so he has to catch me and I run away. You caught me last night. At least I was pretty sure it was you and so then I knew I must go back to David and he would take care of me. So I had my little sickness, but it's over now and it won't happen again for a long time."

When I thanked her for telling me I discovered my throat was so tight the words did not come easily, but I added my promise I would hold her confidence. She looked at me astonished again.

"Why, it's no secret," she said. "I've never tried to hide it. Lots of people have something the matter with them. I'm lucky I'm not crippled. Look how hard I can work. And another thing, David's as mad about animals as I am and he's wonderful with them."

She got up and walked to the door.

"You see," she said, "I'm really quite, quite healthy. By the way," she turned back, "Miranda hasn't birthed yet but David's keeping a close watch on her."

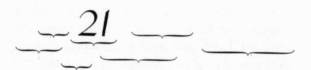

21

IF Sam had not disparaged it with such condescending finality
I doubt that Neill and I would have seen Flogny and the
countryside away from the barge. We moored there about
four o'clock. The day had been sunny and hot. We had spent
the greater part of it on deck watching with pleasure the
landscape unfolding, such time as we were not drowsing.
Romney's quota of the time spent drowsing was as usual the
greatest.

As soon as we had tied up, Sam announced his purpose.
The announcement was unnecessary. His pattern was so well
established we knew that, touching shore, Sam would set off
to find a hospital, if possible, in the vicinity and to have
exercise on a bicycle, usually combining the two projects.
This time, encountering Jenny on his way aft where the bi-

cycles were stored, he invited her to accompany him. They disappeared round a bend of the towpath. Cornelia was the only volunteer to Sophy's call for companionship while she went by taxi to fetch the Volkswagen from St. Florentin. An unexpected spate of rain shooed the stay-at-homes indoors. Frances was concerned about the cyclists. She proposed to Albert that he put on a raincoat, take two others and go by bicycle to find them. Albert was not made happy by the proposal. His eyes widened in alarm.

"Even without a raincoat," he reminded her, "I'm not very good on a bicycle. If I wear one it will either get caught in the chain and throw me or I'll have to hold it up, and I can't do that while I'm steering."

"It wouldn't keep you dry that way either," Frances agreed. "We must think up another plan quickly."

Richard had been putting under cover the chairs on the deck. He came in bringing reassurance. "Don't worry about Jenny and the doctor. They are in a little café. I have learned always to look in a café for passengers who have gone ashore."

Frances was not quite satisfied by this surmise, but when Albert reminded her quickly of postcards to be written she was happily diverted. Romney and I were playing a game of Scrabble when Sam and Jenny returned. The shower was over.

"I want to tell you," Sam announced—he is given rather to announcements than merely passing observations—"we found a delightful little café in the village just as the rain began. We had some coffee and came out dry and warm when the shower was over. However," he added, "I must also tell you this. The village is not worth seeing. Where are Sophy and Cornelia? The Volkswagen isn't here."

I suggested it might have taken them a longer time than usual to retrieve the car. Sam shook his head. "Not at all. We met them and I said the village was not worth seeing. They were just at the outskirts. I thought of course they would be here ahead of us."

Frances looked up from her postcard writing to ask if we thought anything could have happened to them. She was answered by a hail from the General outside and the appearance of Cornelia in the doorway.

"Sophy wants to know if anyone would like to come for a drive. We've been exploring the countryside; it's charming." Neill coming up that moment from his cabin accepted immediately and so did I. Sam smiled indulgently, but said he wanted to read. Frances decided to finish her postcards. Romney would wait for Margalo. She had said she would play solitaire against him after a nap. The others not in sight were presumably sleeping, too. Neill and I agreed not to rouse them. I asked Cornelia if she had a little plan in mind and she looked a bit discomfited.

"Well," she admitted, "I have been thinking that I would try a shower today instead of the tub. I've been working out in my mind a way of making sure my slippers and robe don't get wet if that shower head swivels. I thought I could take a stool."

"It's all right, dear," I interrupted. "You go ahead with your little plan. But, if it's all the same to you, Neill and I will get going. Sophy's waiting."

She stood aside and made a little face at me as I passed her.

When we were in the car Sophy explained to Neill and me what had prompted the detour she and Cornelia had made: "Sheer perversity," and she was a little abashed. "It was Sam's telling us the village was not worth seeing. He was so positive I turned the car right round and drove through it. As a matter of fact he was right, the village itself isn't much, but wait till you see what it depends on."

The reason for the existence of the village must be the

magnificent château it fringes. We could only catch glimpses of the house itself set far back from the road. A winding driveway leads to it, with broad lawns on either side. Magnificent old trees outline the driveway and the lawns. Beyond them the buildings of the working farm are more visible than the château itself. Most of these are in the center of green fields, slashed of course by one of mustard. Beyond this estate, that is, as Brother would say, *formidable* in size, the road curves and we found ourselves unexpectedly driving through a forest. This was a landscape we had not seen since we had left the forest of Fontainebleau. We were reasonably sure the road would eventually bring us out of the woods, but we had not anticipated it would deliver us back to the beginning of the château property. We were far more surprised, however, to see a familiar figure coming toward us across a field. We asked one another incredulously if that could be Frances and agreed it was. The recent heavy shower had turned the ground to mud. At each step her feet sank well over the shoe tops. The sight of us startled her a little, enough to send her momentarily off balance. When she lifted a foot again for the next step the shoe did not come with it. She retrieved but did not put it on again. A bunch of dispirited wild flowers drooped over her other hand. She noticed their condition when she waved to us and when she reached the car explained ruefully:

"I should have got them into water sooner, they were so lovely, but the mud held me back."

She refused with fierce stubbornness to be driven to the barge. "I will not put mud in the car."

"Albert is going to have a wonderful time," she added, and explained what had seemed to me a striking non sequitur. "He loves to clean shoes. He says at heart he's always been a bootblack. He carries equipment I'm sure is more complete and elaborate than theirs. This pair will really give him a wonderful time."

The barge was not far away but we drove a little beyond it to complete our circuit. Returning we saw Albert on the deck. He was sitting crosslegged, shoeshining paraphernalia around him and so absorbed he did not notice us until we had climbed aboard and stood beside him. He held up the shoe on which he was working.

"A present from Frances," he said.

Life inside the barge had not the quality of serenity Albert's blissful preoccupation had led us to expect. Jenny returning from her bicycle excursion with Sam had discovered the stowaway cat was, as Jenny called it, "birthing," and Jenny had turned midwife. As we came though the doors into the saloon her head popped up over the top of the ladder from the crews' quarters below and aft.

"Second one here," she announced with proprietary triumph, "all black, quite healthy, more to come."

Her head vanished from sight. She returned to her and the cat's labor. Except for this moment's distraction, Brother and Emily seemed to be the center of attention from the company that was complete now with our arrival, excluding the bootblack.

"I was just saying," Brother explained, "Emily and I got to talking things over this afternoon and decided we're going to run out on you and go to Paris Monday."

The others had just heard the announcement. They nodded in mournful corroboration.

"It's your fault, Sam," I told him to his visible astonishment. "Yes, it is," I repeated. "If you hadn't said the village wasn't worth seeing, Emily and Brother would have gone to see it. They wouldn't have had time on their hands to cook up this dreadful idea." Honesty made me add with reluctance, "Of course, you're perfectly right. It's the thing to do."

Sam alternately spluttered his innocence and berated himself. He had thought it a mild observation but it had sent Sophy careening with recruits through the countryside merely to refute him and now evidently he was responsible for a break in the ranks—a leak in the dike, and he had been responsible. One of the first things a doctor learns, he said, is not to share an opinion unless called in consultation.

Emily soothed him. It had been entirely her idea; Sam and the village had nothing whatever to do with it. She had mentioned to Brother the only tiny flaw in the entire trip was the skimpy time allowed for Paris. She had never seen it. Brother for years had wanted to return, with her, and Brother had said, "Well, why don't we?" So he had consulted Richard, learned there was an express to Paris from Tonnerre, that we would reach tomorrow, Sunday. They could leave the day after, Monday morning. We would be coming up on Thursday, they would miss only three days on the barge, but think what those days would mean in Paris.

"Third kitten," Jenny called from the ladder, "quite healthy. I think it's the last," and disappeared.

Neill laughed, "It's an omen," he said, "three kittens, three days in Paris, quite healthy."

22

RAIN in the morning and the news the château would be closed on Monday are the only reasons I can give for our visiting Tanlay wearing slacks, sneakers and head covering that ranged from scarves to my rain hat Cornelia had appropriated and wore rakishly. The rain had stopped by midafternoon and the sun was bright and hot, but at noon when we moored at Tonnerre we were in a heavy downpour. We were happy to be indoors and happily engaged in our respective and by this time established activities when Richard interrupted. He had come to tell us apologetically he had found it necessary to tie up at Tonnerre in order to make inquiries about conditions ahead. He had heard rumors there was some repair work being made on the canal that would make necessary a change of route. He thought we would be on our way again within two hours proceeding to Tanlay, where we would moor for the night. He suggested we might like to take advantage of the stop to retrieve the car from Flogny and bring it on to Tanlay. He suggested further, since Tonnerre was the station from which Emily and Brother would take the train next day to Paris, they might go to the station, confirm the departure time and buy their tickets. The station was only a short distance away. He would show it to them from the deck.

Brother and Emily thought this a sound idea and went below for raincoats. The General, who had only once yielded her place at the wheel and had never let pass an opportunity for exercise, said she would like a walk into the town to find a taxi and would go for the car in Flogny. Neill volunteered at once to accompany her. Cornelia scarcely looked up from her needlepoint. She was not interested she said in going through the rain to see a railway station nor find a taxi. Margalo and Romney, deep in their individual games of solitaire back to back, neither looked up nor spoke. Unlike Romney, who eschewed it whenever possible, Sam could usually be counted on to join any expedition that promised exercise. He did not disappoint us, either by refusing a chance to walk or by following his very particular direction. He had been happily surprised to find we were making an unexpected stop at Tonnerre because in the guidebook he had read that at Tonnerre there was a very old hospital and had been sorry not to see it. To have it practically dropped in his lap made him jubilantly impatient to be on his way. Not one of the three prospects, taxi, railway station nor hospital, pleased me, but I had my own source of jubilation. I had found on the bookshelves a detective story I had not previously read.

Frances and Albert, at their writing table, of course, were wistful.

"If we thought we could get money," Frances explained,

"we wouldn't walk, we'd run all the way, but it's Sunday. Everything closed. All those days of Ascension," she added bitterly, "and then on the heels of it, Sunday."

For several days the Hacketts had been vociferously in straitened circumstances. They had no money and they could get no money, they had complained indignantly. With equal

indignation they refused a loan. They had been equally vehement in flouting a suggestion that the collapse of their economy had been brought about by their profligate investment in postcards. The reason for their financial embarrassment, they had assured us earnestly and frequently, was a reluctance to carry a sizable amount of money. They liked to cash traveler's checks as they went along, but who would have dreamed, they asked rhetorically, that at our leisurely pace, though they loved it, we would leave too early, arrive too late, or be met with holidays as well as Sundays.

Richard had left after his bulletin. He came back to tell us we were moored, the gangplank was down and those who were leaving could go at any time. Hearing the last of Frances' plaint he knew the substance of it. He had heard it before.

"There is no holiday tomorrow," he promised her. "When you drive Mr. and Mrs. Kimbrough back here to Tonnerre to catch their train you can cash a check."

Albert asked if Richard would be willing to swear to that, and Richard grinning said he would.

Within twenty minutes of leaving, Emily and Brother were back on the barge again, wet and disgruntled. We were as they left us, in the same positions, the same occupations, and startled at their returning so soon. Frances, with characteristically immediate concern, asked if they'd been unable to find the station.

"We found it," Brother told her grimly. "It's closed on Sunday."

In less than an hour Sam had returned to us as close to fuming as perhaps I shall ever see that equable man. Again it was Frances who voiced concern. Had he not been able to find the hospital?

"Without the slightest difficulty," he said and erupted into incredulous indignation.

"I couldn't get in," he said. "I couldn't get in," repeating it with an encircling gesture of his arm that urged us to share the incredibility of such a thing. "I rang the bell. No one came. The door had a large glass panel inset. I could see through it a young woman, receptionist, clerk, whatever she was. She was at a desk writing. I knocked on the glass, she looked up, looked down again and went on writing. I knocked again. I may even have pounded a little," he admitted sheepishly. "She didn't even look up. I could see glass doors beyond her and on the other side of them the wards.

There were patients in wheelchairs. I cupped my hands around my mouth and pressed against the glass and called, 'Je suis un docteur.' That young woman heard me, she had to hear me.''

"She didn't come to the door?" Frances suggested sympathetically.

"Come to the door! She didn't even stop writing. I saw no doctors about, no interest. What kind of a hospital is this? Do they lock it up on Sundays?"

"I expect so," was Albert's comment, "and on saints' days too, just like banks. You can't get money and you can't get sick.''

Sam turned away, wanting to get into dry things, he said. Possibly hoping to distract him from his discomfiture, Frances called after him: "Did you see the *old* hospital?"

He had reached the top of the stairs. Turning back to us with a slow dignity that produced something of a Shakespearean quality he answered her.

"That hospital," he said, "has already been closed for several hundred years."

A little before his two-hour limit was reached Richard came back from his conference. He came into the saloon, obviously in a hurry.

"I must push off at once," he told us, "if we're to reach Tanlay before the château closes. Is everyone accounted for?"

Margalo looked up briefly, a card in her hand. "Yes," she said. "Just don't ask them to give an accounting," and returned to her game.

The sky cleared after lunch and as we came out on deck a meadowlark rose into it, sending down from his invisibility a waterfall of song. This was reason enough, I decided on the instant, not to go down to my cabin for even long enough time to change from my rainy-weather clothes. It must have been a unanimous decision tacitly arrived at, because everyone settled on the deck. The countryside newly washed was sparkling. Other birds were singing. Their music lulled Romney almost immediately into a happy doze; he was smiling as he slept. Neill, leaving with Sophy to get the car, had dropped into my lap a sheet of notepaper.

"These are some things I've been jotting down," he told me, "that I've noticed especially on this trip and loved."

Reading it, I marveled again at Neill's wide knowledge, keen observation and capacity for absorbing and enjoying every prospect. It is a memorandum I could not have made. It reads:

"The rich and varied bird life along the Yonne River and the Burgundy Canal, especially songbirds.

"The chaffinch and blackbird sing throughout the day. Pied wagtails and great tits are common. Magpies, swallows and carrion crows are wherever there are thick woods, especially pines. Have frequently seen green woodpeckers. Their flight is undulating. Have seen one heron very much like the great blue heron in the U.S.A. One large dark hawk we would call a buzzard. Very surprised to see in this region spotted sandpipers. Have heard number of cuckoos, difficult to see. One nightingale and numbers of nightjars—cousin of the U.S.A. whippoorwill. Binoculars essential on trip of this sort both for birdwatching and scenery. Should also bring book—*A Field Guide to the Birds of Britain and Europe* by Roger Tory Peterson."

Frances, settled in a steamer chair with book and compass, interrupted my reading with a sharp exclamation of dismay. "Oh dear, I hadn't realized we have to be at the Tanlay château before four or we won't get in."

Romney opened one eye. "Closes at four?" he inquired.

"Yes," Frances answered and, smiling acidly, added, "and all day Monday." She became at once an aide-de-camp to the General, who was not there. She hurried us ashore the instant we were moored. She started us off across the fields toward the towers we could see just beyond. We did not realize until we reached the gate she was not with us. She had risked missing the tour in order to tell Sophy and Neill the need for haste.

Sophy told us later they were surprised to see Frances. "She was in the middle of the road beckoning, when we drove up."

Seeing her agitation, Sophy's immediate conjectures had ranged from drowning to a fire, as she put on the brakes.

"The others are waiting at the gates," Frances had explained with her head at the window of the car. "You must come right away. You can park the car there and go back to the barge later."

"The château's about to close?" Neill suggested.

"Of course," was her answer, "need you ask? And *all day* tomorrow."

They joined us at the gate as Cornelia was finishing reading aloud the account in the guidebook of the château. From this we had learned the château was built about 1550 and is counted one of the finest examples of the French Renaissance. During the Wars of Religion Huguenot conspirators held their meetings in one of its towers. There are two staircase towers marking two wings, each at right angles to the main building, and each ending in a round tower surmounted by a dome and, on that, a small lantern tower. The approach to the château is across the Cour Verte ("Green Courtyard"). This is almost entirely surrounded by arches framing lovely vistas of garden and woods. The side of the courtyard without arches has instead a bridge crossing a moat and ending at the great doorway that in turn opens to the court of the inner court of honor.

We need not have rushed. There was a chain across the door to the interior guarded by a female Cerberus of a strain that only France seems to produce. These creatures can never have been children. They come out of cracks in walls and they are old. Immediately on their appearance they are put to work as ushers in the National Theater, as guardians of historic monuments, and in private industry as concierges of dwellings. Because of their long chrysalis period underground their eyesight is poor. This makes it difficult for those who are ushers to read the seat location on a theatre ticket, habitually causing both delay and a general re-seating to correct errors. They have, however, an acute tactile sense and can detect the instant it touches the palm the denomination of the coin that has been placed there and respond accordingly, always noisily. Their hearing is poor, too. They do not understand questions asked of them and probably because of their deafness their voices are louder and brassier than those of a human being.

This member of the species, stooped, fat, wrinkled, semi-toothless, bawled at us to remain at the door where she stood until a preceding tour was completed and its members came out.

"Watch Neill," Sophy cautioned. "In a minute he'll have her showing photographs of her relatives in America and he'll tell us later she was a dear thing and probably a beauty at one time."

Neill was smiling indulgently and a little sheepishly, when on the instant, before our eyes the gentle bird and flower lover turned into the Admiral. Striding forward, he grasped the concierge by the arm and, indicating the barrier with his other hand, thundered, "Open that at once. Here comes the United States Ambassador," and in the same breath called out sunnily, "Hi, Chip."

"Merciful God," Cornelia said in my ear, "look at us, the raggle-taggle gypsies."

We met and chatted with Ambassador and Mrs. Bohlen,

who were spending the weekend in the vicinity. They were the only people we met on the cruise that any of us knew and the only time on the cruise we were ashore not only unsuitably dressed but unpressed, mud-spattered—a down-at-the-heels bunch of Sunday trippers. The Bohlens were charming, affable and very suitably dressed.

Discussing it at dinner that night, we agreed that though the exterior was spectacular, the furnishings of the château were not to our liking. It is possible our eyes were jaundiced by discomfiture at our own appearance.

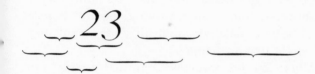

23

"OH no, madame," the hotel clerk in Tonnerre said, "the bank is not open."

"It is Monday," Frances reminded him.

"Ah yes, madame, but it is a special day."

Frances lifted her arm and I thought she was going to strike him, but she slapped her own forehead instead and without a word turned on her heel and walked out of the lobby, Albert following. Sophy, Cornelia and I were waiting in the courtyard. Through the open doorway we had heard the news, but when the Hacketts came out we thought it best to make no comment. Frances strode past us—she usually strolled—with an expression befitting Clytemnestra.

Albert tarried long enough to confide in a low tone and shielding his mouth, "The bank is closed."

Sophy mouthed back at him, "We know, we heard."

Cornelia and I shook commiserating heads. Sophy had raised her voice, I think because she wanted not to try Frances further by seeming to talk behind her back.

Frances stopped as abruptly as if she had been given a military command to halt.

"Albert," she said, pointing dramatically, "look!"

We looked, with him.

"Do you see that sign right there down that little street? 'Bureau de Change.' That means a place where you change money, and I'll bet," she added, "they have no saints there."

Albert volunteered immediately to go alone and Frances was grateful. "If they make any difficulty," she explained, "I'm afraid I might lose my temper."

We saw Albert on his way and returned to the railway station, where we had dropped Emily and Brother to buy their tickets and check their baggage. They were still involved in the undertaking. The ticket agent had just opened his window, explaining he had been having his lunch and that the baggage men having not quite finished would be along presently.

Leaving the ticket buyers to put their French into use, we went outside again. The view over the countryside was charming. In Tonnerre almost all buildings are in close proximity and within view of one another. As the guidebook says: "Tonnerre is a pleasant little town terraced on one of the hills that form the left bank of the Armançon, and is surrounded by vineyards and green scenery, population 5,760."

I must interpolate that, considering its dimensions, I cannot understand why there was scarcely a sign post we had read since the beginning of the trip, not only along the waterways but far inland, that did not include directions to Tonnerre. The only other place in the world I know that is so ubiquitous is Danbury, Connecticut.

We saw Albert hurrying toward us.

Frances greeted him eagerly, arms outstretched and with one word, "Money!"

Albert shook his head; Frances did not strike him; she shook him. He was acutely embarrassed about his news, but he spoke with courageous honesty.

"The place is open," he said directly to Frances. "I'm sure we'll get a check cashed, but the fact is," he paused, swallowed, resumed, "there's a very large fierce dog and he's loose." Albert swallowed again. "I looked in the door! It wasn't locked, so the place must be open, but I didn't see anybody, only this big dog that jumped on me. I called but nobody answered. I did have the door closed by that time. I'm not very good about dogs," he added wistfully.

Sophy, Cornelia and I volunteered to go back with him. As dog lovers we said we might not antagonize the mastiff or whatever he was, and we promised Frances we would not take any chances. We would open the door only a little, and if he came at us we would close it and call. Surely whoever was there—and there must be someone—would hear three people at the door. We urged Frances to stay. She had found her temper but was losing it again. Eyes flashing, she delivered a pithy statement about ways in this country of keeping people from getting money.

"If it's not saints," she declared, "they employ savage dogs."

In the end Cornelia and I persuaded her and Sophy to stay. The General could soothe Frances and lend a hand with Emily and Brother, who might be floundering about in unfamiliar vocabulary. Cornelia and I walked back with Albert to the Bureau de Change. The dog did jump at us the moment we opened the door. He was big for a springer spaniel and he must have been about four months old, all paws and slobbering affection. He galloped dementedly around us, skidding on the smooth floor when we pushed him away.

"À bas," I commanded. It seemed to me as I used it a pompous expression but I could think of no other synonym for "down."

We were making enough noise, I would have thought, to bring in the entire citizenry of Tonnerre, but our only catch was the clerk of the Bureau de Change. He had been having his lunch and had not wished to be disturbed.

He eyed us reproachfully as he lifted a napkin tucked under and halfway round his collar, and wiped his mouth. Released, the napkin hung limp and damp down over his stomach. (I do not know why this is so but it is a generalization I can safely make from my experience in France: table-cloths and napkins are always damp.)

Perhaps he thought we had come in to have a romp with his puppy because he turned away and started back to the inner room, but Cornelia called to him it was a question of *affaires* for which we had come.

Sighing unhappily, he left the threshold of his sanctuary and assumed his official place behind the counter. He was in his shirt sleeves, each sleeve encircled by a rubber band that held the cuffs well above the wrists to prevent, of course, soiling and fraying. He removed the napkin from under his chin, folded it carefully first, then rolled it and inserted it into a napkin ring he drew from beneath the counter. I had not noticed, in the far corner, a plain wooden table and chair until the clerk walked over to them, loosed from the chair back a thin and shiny black alpaca coat. He put this on as he walked back, settling the collar and sleeves carefully in place and patting the pockets to make sure, I suppose, of their contents.

This bit of housekeeping attended to, he placed both hands on the counter, leaned forward and requested us to state the nature of our affairs. Cornelia on the other side leaning forward, too, as close to his ear as she could reach, suggested hoarsely our matters might be more easily arranged if the dog were put in the back room. I think Albert was patting the spaniel's head to show good fellowship but since at the moment of contact his hand jerked back convulsively the mammoth mistook this for an invitation to catch it and with maniacally shrill yelps of excitement and uncoordinated leaps was endeavoring to accept the invitation. The clerk shook his head regretfully but with some pride.

"It is a strong character," he said, "though amiable. But when he is alone he is not so amiable, because he is not happy. So do you see he eats things," he paused, "everything," he added reminiscently. "He cannot be put in the other room."

From under the counter where there was evidently a storage place for a diversity of personal accessories, the clerk brought a kind of thong about eight inches long, solid and braided in a variety of colors. I think it had been homemade from cast-off stockings.

"If madame would care to present this to Bijou," he said, handing it across the countertop to me, "he will accept it with pleasure and become quite tranquil."

I tapped Albert on the arm with it. "I'll take over here," I told him. "I've brought a pacifier."

I have never been at an oasis when a traveler crawled to it from the desert but I imagine he would look at the water much as Albert looked at me. We executed an involuntary and spontaneous dance figure a spectator might have thought was Spanish. With my hands lifted high above my head, the thong between, I clucked at Bijou, calling his attention. Albert at the same moment in a series of short running steps went around me and to the counter, on which he immediately and heavily leaned.

Bijou responded to my clucking. He sat down, his tongue

and a good deal of saliva dripping from one corner of his mouth, and looked up expectantly at the pacifier. I lowered it and myself to the ground. He engulfed one end in his mouth, but I held on to the other. The purpose of this had not been a game of fetch but a soporific and it worked. Bijou lay quiet, munching with slobbering pleasure. I could then give my attention to the transaction at the counter. Albert had torn from his book an American Express check, signed it and was at the moment of my attention extending it to the clerk.

"I would like to cash it," he said. "It is for $50."

From the upper right-hand pocket of his alpaca coat the bank clerk drew a spectacles case and took out steel-rimmed glasses. After blowing on each lens he polished them with a handkerchief taken from the left-hand breast pocket still folded. From where I sat on the floor I had an impression that from the time it had been placed there the handkerchief had never been unfolded. The spectacles on and adjusted with settling of the side pieces and considerable nose twitching, the banker took Albert's check and read every word written on it, moving his lips but making no sound.

Looking up at the completion of his perusal he said in French, "Unhappily I do not speak or read English but will you permit me to inquire, is this paper genuine?"

Cornelia assured him it was genuine, very well known and credited throughout the world.

"Without doubt," was his answer, "but you will pardon me, I must confirm it. A very little moment if you please."

He retreated to the back room. We listened to his end of a telephone conversation, Cornelia translating rapidly and happily to Albert.

"Monsieur, my chief," he began, "I am engaged in a very great work, with very distinguished American clients."

"That's what $50 has made of you!" Cornelia inserted in her translation.

"The very distinguished American gentleman has presented me a paper with the title on it The American Express" (that was a joy to hear). "He tells me it is to the amount of $50 and this is indeed true because I am looking at the numbers. He wishes that I should take this paper and give him francs. It is permitted? Yes, he has made the signature. I inquire only if the American Express" (double treat) "is genuine and to be honored. Ah, it is so. Then I shall make my computations, I thank you. You are very kind. Again I thank you, good-bye."

He was smiling when he returned to us.

"Aha," he said, "so everything is as it is necessary. Now I make the calculations."

The storage shelves under the counter produced a thick writing pad made up of papers in assorted sizes, colors and textures, held together by a string through a hole punched in the top of each. He took this over to the table and chair in the corner where his coat had hung, sat down and began his calculations with the equipment I have found standard in every post office and bank in France, the scratchiest pens in all Christendom. The pen squeaked and splattered its way over a number of pages that were torn off and thrown on the floor until, arriving at an accounting that suited him, our international financier returned with the paper.

"I have now the amount," he told us. "I will bring you the francs."

He was in the inner room long enough for us to exchange surmises about how many vaults he had to open before actual money could be reached. Returning he counted in our presence the sum he had brought and gestured to it proudly.

"There, monsieur, is your $50, making twenty francs."

"Thank you very much," Albert said, and at the banker's indication shook hands with him across the counter. The banker assured him not at all, not at all, it had been a great pleasure.

As he opened his billfold Albert looked at the notes again, counted them, turned toward Cornelia and me (Cornelia said afterward, "At that moment he looked like Parsifal, the guileless knight"), and said timidly, "You know I think twenty francs is not quite right. Oughtn't it be more than that? I'm sure Frances will think so."

We were startled.

Releasing my hold of the thong—and happily Bijou did not notice this—I counted on my fingers and exploded. "Albert, I should think it isn't right. Fifty dollars is two hundred and fifty francs."

"My God," Albert prayed, "now what do we do?"

Cornelia, lifting a commanding hand to us, addressed herself to the banker in French, of course.

"Monsieur," she said, "I must ask you to consider something."

"Yes, madame," he agreed.

"Now then," she drew a deep breath. "Figure to yourself this, and look on your chart. One hundred dollars equals five hundred francs, is it not so, does it not say that?"

"Excuse me a very little moment," was his answer. He retired to the inner room, and came back with an official chart of exchange. He spread this on the counter top, brought a forefinger slowly down to statements of currencies until it rested on the American exchange.

"You have indeed reason," he assured Cornelia, "five hundred francs equals one hundred dollars."

She drew another deep breath. "Very well, monsieur, since that is so and since fifty is one half of one hundred, without doubt fifty dollars is one half of a hundred dollars, is that not so?" The banker nodded.

Now she was a feminine Caruso in chest expansion.

"The fifty dollars, being one-half of one hundred dollars is one-half of the five hundred francs that is one hundred dollars. It is in effect two hundred and fifty francs, no?"

The banker looked across at her long and earnestly before he spoke.

"It is that it is so," he said at last, and then shrugged. "It is a little mistake that. But now do you see I must extract a little sum for the service I have performed in the exchange, that is indeed the law."

That cost Albert twenty francs, $4. To this day Frances voices her outraged resentment of the charge.

"Albert was duped," she says.

Cornelia likes to talk about her financial triumph.

"I saw immediately or almost immediately," she will tell you, "that since fifty dollars was half of one hundred it was bound to be half the number of francs a hundred dollars would be, and I knew what that was. Still I do think it's remarkable," she usually adds ruminatively, "considering I once got 'two' in a mathematics exam for being present."

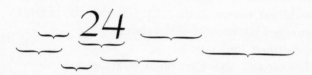

24

COMING back to Tanlay exhausted, we agreed that for us Tonnerre was exactly the right name for the town we hoped not to see again. Thereafter we referred to the episodes as the things that happened at Thunder.

The initial shock that banks were closed that day, the trying experience at the exchange, Cornelia's Aristotelian logic that rescued Albert—these episodes had been trying and harrowing, but Emily's and Brother's departure had not been without incident. More than once while the banker was making his calculations we had wailed to one another our despair that we would not be at the station to wave them off, but each of us was essential to the transaction. To our happy surprise on our return to the station we had learned the train was due in fifteen minutes. Someone, it could not have been

Cornelia, had made a slight miscalculation in the reading of the train schedule. Brother had purchased the tickets with no difficulty, he told Cornelia proudly, and had found a porter to whom the luggage had been consigned.

"When I saw that porter," Emily interjected, "I could have kissed him for being so typical. He had on a washed-out blue smock, a beret and a cigarette smoked down to nothing but an ember, attached to his lower lip."

They were both in a state of euphoria. Brother was smiling vacantly and looking not very bright, and Emily was saying repeatedly, "You know this train ride is a great adventure for us."

The Hacketts had not been in our little group at the station. Albert had gone immediately to tell Frances of the events at the exchange and show her proof of solvency restored, and at sight of it Frances had immediately led the way from the station to an objective we did not know but could guess.

From far down the track a spatter of piercing shrill and staccato whistles had sent ahead the news the train was coming. That sound always invokes for me the image of a woman who has just seen a mouse. Emily laughed like a child.

"Oh," she told us, "it's exactly the way you said it would sound."

The stationmaster had come out on the platform in a resplendent uniform and a majesty of bearing appropriate to it. He had answered the train's salute with peals of equal decibels from a silver whistle at the end of a long silver chain around his neck. Since he was standing alongside us when he delivered this cadenza he had taken, temporarily, our hearing, so that we could only guess and partially lip-read that in a flurry of embraces we were saying how wonderful the trip had been, how we would miss one another, how we would be together again soon in Paris.

In spite of deafness I had been aware Cornelia was speaking with such agitation and emotion as to seem excessive until she resorted to a brilliant pantomime. Stooping down and seeming to carry in either hand a heavy suitcase, she had made us realize Emily and Brother were boarding the train without their luggage. It was on the platform some distance from us. Brother had left the train to the angry astonishment of passengers endeavoring to board it. Emily had followed him lest she be abandoned. My appeal to the stationmaster to hold the train was pitched no lower than his whistle had been. His response had been a gesture of command I have seen in pictures of Roman emperors. The train had waited, the baggage had been gathered up, the Kimbroughs had returned to the train, boarded it.

Albert and Frances had arrived at the foot of the steps to the travelers' compartment a little breathless, but blowing kisses, waving, calling their messages—the train whistle shrieked, so did the stationmaster's, and the Kimbroughs were on their way to Paris.

As we had turned to leave Frances had asked apologetically if we would wait just a minute. They had left a few things when they had run to the train to say their good-byes. There were postcards spread out over the surface of an empty baggage truck. In the money again they had set out immediately for the day's purchase, and on their return to the station had found the baggage truck an excellent desk at which, standing, to write.

As we came in sight of the barge Cornelia sighed deeply.

"Thank God," she said, "the lights of Dover. Home again." She smiled dreamily. "I'm going straight to the deck. I'm going to lie there all day. Perhaps someone will bring me lunch: if he does I hope he won't speak to me."

"That's what you think," Sophy told her inelegantly. "The deck is occupied. Dr. and Mrs. Benard are there."

Cornelia's answer was a threat to remain in the car. She was persuaded, not easily, to leave it; but when we reached the Benards she was graciousness itself. Standing a little behind her I whispered this in her ear and was rewarded by a sharp back kick in the shins. Margalo was smiling brightly and listening attentively but at the sight of us crossed her eyes imploringly, continuing to smile. Romney was listening too and so were the Benards, but Sam was talking easily with no pause for words, his gestures acting as interpreter. At the sight of us he broke off what he was saying, and whatever that was I had not yet become attuned to. I came in squarely on the beam however when he continued.

"Ici are votre other amis. Except for Mr. and Mrs. Kimbrough who have left nous to aller à Paris."

We shook hands all round of course, and sat down to discuss plans for the day. Cornelia headed for a deckchair but I forestalled her by sitting on the end of it. Dr. Benard was insistent that we visit the little town of Ancy-le-Libre; it was charming; he wanted his wife to see it. When this was conveyed to Margalo she was recalcitrant.

"Why doesn't he drive his wife over there some Sunday then?" she muttered. "He says it took them no time at all to get here in their car; it's taken us since last Friday, and I don't feel I have to push on."

The instant we were moored, charmingly, to an apple tree, Dr. Benard organized and took charge of the expedition. Judging by an expression of vacuity on her face, I think the General was stupefied. When she followed him docilely off the boat, I knew she was in shock.

The two doctors went ahead in the doctor's car, Mrs. Benard in our Microbus. Mrs. Benard explained her choice of car. Sophy, repeating it to me later, added advice not to pass this on to Margalo. Mrs. Benard had said, "We often come here so I know the route very well." She had joined Sophy in order to show the way, though that had been the doctor's purpose.

"My husband is such a fast driver he will be out of your sight in two minutes. Do not try to keep up with him."

They left the Microbus at Ancy-le-Libre and returned to the barge in the doctor's car. Sophy said Mrs. Benard had not underestimated his driving. She had never been so frightened in her life—a motoring admission I would have thought I could never hear from the General. The confession had evidently made her uncomfortable, too, because she had justified it irritably.

"It's not only that he drove like a lunatic, and never slowed down for curves or blind crossings, he kept turning around to tell me how advantageous it was for us to have our car waiting at Ancy-le-Libre; we would never find a taxi in so small a village. Of course I'll have to drive him back to Tanlay to pick up his own car; he didn't mention that."

Sam did not make a speech at lunch, but he directed the conversation at his end of the table, where the doctor was seated. He did not monopolize it but his method of keeping it general was direct and effective.

"I think the doctor would be interested in the techniques developed by our anesthetists," was one of his suggestions, "and the types of anesthesia we are using."

Smiling benignly at the doctor, he would flash to him the key word anesthetic, then turn back to the rest of us. The rest of us included Sophy, Romney and me, and our only experience in this field had been as unhappy recipients of the method of inducing unconsciousness. Explaining this to Sam with overlapping insistence only brought his benign smile in our direction.

"I will explain it," he reassured us. "You have only to put it in French when I do not make myself entirely clear."

I longed for Brother; I would have given almost anything to have had him in my place at that moment. It would have been a sweet revenge for something he had done to me years before. The recollection of it flashed into my memory. We had been on a family motor trip in France and Brother had sat in front beside the chauffeur. Every day he had demanded of me such things as the French for camshaft, or, "Ask Louis if the differential is . . ." God knows what, since I do not know today any more about what a differential does or is than I did then. When I protested my ignorance of these things, Brother would point out furiously to my father what a total waste of money my education had been.

Sam was not angered by the exposure of our inadequacies, but when we endeavored to move the talk into channels in which we could be articulate he would firmly take the wheel again and steer us back to the operating room.

At the other end of the table Cornelia was at the helm. I do not wish to belittle her accomplishment in steering a course through bright inanities with little or no assistance, but proficient as she is in the language I do maintain her assignment was easier than ours. She could choose the subject and Madame Benard was charmingly responsive. Dr. Benard was charming but since we ourselves did not know what we were saying it was impossible to know if he was responding. Cornelia's companions in the group around Madame Benard were Margalo, Frances, Albert and Neill. I could hear Neill put in a phrase now and then but there were no words from the Hacketts nor Margalo; only from Frances, who is the most polite and considerate woman I know, an intermittent humming sound. It was a kind of song without words I think was meant to convey general warmth, hospitality and an assurance she was listening and agreeing with whatever it was Madame Benard and Cornelia were saying. Whenever I looked in their direction Margalo was smiling at Madame Benard with an intensity that ought to have frightened the daylights out of her.

At some time during lunch Richard had cast off but Madame Benard evidently had not realized we were moving. I heard her exclaim with happy surprise the landscape through the windows facing her was changing. Frances hummed an acquiescence to this observation. Margalo's smile did not change. Albert looked up from his food to say, "Ah," and Neill ventured a sally in French to the effect that it did not change rapidly, and this brought appreciative laughter from Madame Benard and Cornelia. I returned my attention from that sparkling conversation to Sam's need of the French equivalent for sodium pentothal. There were moments during the meal when I reasoned with myself empirically that since, on every other day during the cruise, lunch had come to an end I could assure myself this one would too. There were moments when I felt the assumption would not be justified, but empiric reasoning triumphed.

A little before three o'clock we arose from the table. At the same moment Richard and David were tying up the boat at Ancy-le-Libre. As we came on deck Richard suggested we visit a mill in the vicinity, within easy walking distance. We found it without difficulty and were welcomed first by the wife of the owner and then by the jolly miller himself. I thought with immediate satisfaction he was exactly as he should be, coated with flour from head to foot and smiling jovially through it. The mill itself was run almost entirely by machinery, requiring only three operators, the miller, his wife and one assistant. We climbed a circular open wooden staircase without so much as a handrail in order to be shown every detail of the process and all the wheels in motion. What with feeling I had been hurtled once more into a world of camshafts and differentials or whatever, and my feeling of giddiness from a height no greater than the top of a kitchen stepladder, I was glad when my foot touched the ground floor again. I had come down the stairs backward.

For all the machinery inside, the exterior of the building was as happily in character as the miller himself. It was of timber and stone covered with vines and built over a mill-race. We stood a few minutes on a diminutive stone arched bridge to watch the rushing stream beneath and turned our back on a delivery truck that roared in, but not before we had seen painted on its side the advertisement of a local bakery. I thought it nice a bakery should get flour direct from the mill but would have liked it to be called for in a horse-drawn two-wheeled cart.

Following Richard's directions we continued along the road past the mill, crossed the canal over a stone bridge and came into the village itself. I have seen prettier villages and more beautiful gardens but I have never seen a garden that touched me so deeply as the one beside the church. It is small, perhaps thirty feet square, completely walled, entered by a gate in the middle of one of them; but within the garden the walls are totally effaced by magnificent topiary so exquisitely precise the garden must receive tender loving care and daily attention. I realized it was a memorial garden when I saw a shaft in the center covered with names. They were of the men from that village killed in the last war. Though the shaft is more than six feet high the names cover every inch of it. The only other garden ornament was a shell case in each of the four corners. Artificial flowers were set in them but live ones grew around the base. I was looking at the names on the shaft when Neill came through the gate. As usual we had all separated somewhere along the road from the mill. I suppose Sam had remained with the Benards but I had not known anyone had come into the garden after me until I heard and recognized the voice that followed a loud gasp.

"My God! What topiary!"

If I had been surprised and touched by the hidden garden I had discovered, Neill, the topiary expert, was staggered by the sight he had come upon. He had not been speaking to me; he had not known I was there until I said, "Isn't it sweet and touching?"

"Sweet?" he echoed. "Why those yews are at least a hundred and fifty years old. Magnificent is what they are."

When I showed him the names and dates on the shaft in the center of the garden and pointed out the shell cases filled with artificial flowers, he conceded the garden had another quality too. We left it, closing the gate on a mystery we could not solve. What had the yews originally enclosed? Certainly their precise arrangement was not involuntary. Neill was sure they could not have been transplanted, and yet the commemorative shaft and shell cases were of the Second World War. Had this once been a little and special graveyard? And yet if that were so, surely its tombstones would not have been removed. When had the yews been fashioned into topiary? For what purpose had such arduous and specialized work been done and maintained? I doubt that we shall ever know.

Neill was with me when I left the garden, holding the gate open and stopping, I thought, to latch it when we had both gone through. But when I said I saw Frances and Albert down the road seeming to be in a little difficulty I found I was talking into air, emptied of the Admiral.

Frances and Albert were talking to a man and woman. They had looked to be in difficulty because I had seen Frances turn inquiringly to Albert and Albert shake his head. Unlike Neill they welcomed my company. They were in a bit of language trouble, Frances explained, because of a somewhat unusual circumstance. Hearing it, I agreed it was a situation one would not be likely to anticipate. Albert had gone into a little shop, to say for what purpose would be redundant, and while Frances was in the road waiting for him, a man and woman had approached and asked her the time.

"Now you see," Frances told me, "one of the hands on my watch has come off during this trip. I haven't bothered to find a jeweler when we have stopped, to have it put back, because it's only the little hand. During the day I pretty much know what the hour is, so the minute hand is really all I need, especially since Albert wakes me in the morning."

Albert broke in. "She should never have shown her watch to the woman. She could have said, 'I do not have the time,' and she can say that in French."

Frances took over, shaking her head decisively. "It's instinctive. Someone asks you the time and you look at your watch, but I did not know how to say one of the hands has fallen off so they think this is a new American invention, a watch that tells the time with only one hand. They've lost all interest in the actual time. When Albert arrived I asked him to tell them and he did, but they paid no attention. They only want to know about this interesting mechanism." Her voice rose, "And I cannot, I cannot tell them."

The French people were visibly disappointed to learn the reason for the mechanical phenomenon. They themselves were old, the man said unnecessarily, but they liked learning about new things. The woman interrupted eagerly. Would we perhaps have the kindness to teach them a few new things at this moment such as counting in English say up to five and perhaps even the words for yes and no? They had not met Americans before and it would give them happiness and pride to tell how they had been taught to count in English by people from across the ocean in the United States. When we said good-bye they repeated their lesson several times. As long as they were within our hearing we heard them coaching each other in counting up to five and practicing with a nod or shake of the head the correct use of yes and no.

"I have a feeling," Frances said ruminatively, "those dear old people are going to forget about the accident to my watch. They're going to tell the town they've seen a remarkable American invention, a one-handed watch, and each is going to back the other up. They're going to put on a very good show and I'm willing to bet everyone is going to believe whatever they tell."

A sound of drumbeats had reached me, I thought, but I had not given attention either to identify it positively nor wonder at the reason, but a flurry of trumpeted notes that cracked in midair focused my recognition and caught the ears of Frances and Albert too. While we were looking at one another with wild surmise at what might be going on, our erstwhile pupils, out of breath, caught up with us.

"You must go quickly," the old man said, pointing ahead. The old woman nodded vigorously in agreement without speaking. She was holding her hand against a stitch in her side. I told him we would go, of course, but in what honor was the procession? The old woman dropped her hand from her side and with her husband stood as straight as age would concede to them.

"It is the anniversary of our day of liberation," they said in one voice.

Sympathy and tears are swiftly quickened in Frances. When I had translated what the old man said she nodded a few times and, putting her hand on the old woman's shoulder, spoke directly to both in English.

"Now," she said with a catch in her voice and her eyes brimming, "I forgive the banks for closing today."

She and Albert hurried in the direction of the band; the couple followed more slowly. I ran back along the way we had come, pausing to look through the garden gate in case some of the others had found it. I did not want them to miss the big event. After a few minutes I gave up. I saw no reason to miss it myself. I am nothing like so unselfish as Frances.

The parade was not much larger than the memorial garden where it ended, but when I arrived there, its size had been augmented by four, the old couple and the Hacketts, marching arm in arm.

The sound had rounded up the others. We met at the gate. We did not wait for whatever ceremony took place inside; there would not have been room for us in any case. Frances and Albert dropped out. We were now full strength of the company, with the exception, of course, of Neill, whom we found on our return to the barge at his accustomed table making notes, guidebooks and maps spread out before him.

The Benards came on board only to say their good-byes but Sam insisted they stay a little while longer. Sophy's eyes glazed.

"There are so many more things to talk about," he said, smiling brightly at those of us who were left; at the moment of his insistence there had occurred a remarkable evaporation. The Hacketts, Margalo and Cornelia were no longer there. They must have been studying prestidigitator Neill's technique for causing himself to disappear, but they needed practice. Whereas his exits were always so silent it was impossible to discover in what direction he had gone, the purpose of the amateurs to head for their cabins was clear. The clatter of feet on the stairs could have come from a subway station in New York at rush hour. Raising his voice above it, Sam addressed himself to Sophy.

"I want to tell the doctor about our program for social security, medical care and other fringe benefits we have established for nurses."

Over his shoulder with happy confidence he was tossing

key words to Dr. Benard—"medical care, social security, welfare." Having established to his satisfaction the tenor of the information to follow, Sam with a gesture invited all of us, those who were left, to sit down. When a man has been presiding over classrooms for forty some years, he knows how to exercise authority. We sat down. Sam continued with Sophy.

"Will you say first that in our social security program . . ."

"No, Sam, I won't." Sophy said afterward no one could have been so surprised as she to hear her say these words. "I'm so tired," she added apologetically. "I've talked so much French today I'm dried up, I'm sorry." Sam translated to the Benards. "Fatigue," he said, "to parler le français." His eyes twinkled suddenly. "Pour moi," he added, "le français does not fatigue."

It was so disarming and immediately comprehensible to the Benards we were all smiling happily at one another as we rose and shook hands all round. Sam was still talking to the Benards as he accompanied them and Sophy to the Volkswagen. I did not hear what he said. I had joined the subway rush to our cabins. I heard Sophy though. Her voice was raised but I did not like the sound of it.

"I'll be thinking of you," she said to us, "all the way to Tanlay and all the way back."

That night by established custom the occupants of the girls' dormitory went to bed first, leaving the men upstairs. This was both to insure right of way for the men to and from the bathroom and to allow us to follow boarding-school tradition: keep our doors open for conversation as we undressed.

It was the first time Emily's door had been closed and we were unhappily and acutely aware of her absence as we reviewed the day. Margalo insisted she was more tired than any of us because she had had to listen to so much French. She was rounded on so vehemently by Cornelia, Sophy and me she was momentarily put to silence, but not for long. Frances was not a participant in these résumés since her cabin was at the other end of the barge. I spoke for her, insisting she had got far more involved than Margalo, and told of her endeavor, into which she had put heart, soul and all the French she knew, to explain to the old couple on the road what time it was by means of a watch with only one hand.

"You know," I said, "how Frances would mourn at not being able to give fully whatever anyone asked. By the time I reached her I think she was ready to sit on the road and pour dust over her head."

When Cornelia and Sophy reiterated the Benards themselves had nothing to do with their exhaustion I agreed wholeheartedly. Both Dr. and Mrs. Benard, I echoed, were charming. It was only the amount and the kind of French that had worn us down.

"As a matter of fact," I told them, "Dr. Benard illuminated the day, or year, or forever, by something he told me and I've been longing for the chance to share it. We were talking about language, I think, idioms, slang, something like that, and he illustrated what he was saying. 'It was like a maid in my mother's house,' he told me. 'My mother discovered the girl was pregnant and was horrified and furious. She gave the girl the devil, told her she had always thought her respectable, good, and was bitterly disappointed. The maid cried, of course, and then she said to my mother, "Madame, truly I am a good girl. I have always been a good girl. This situation is due to only a very little moment of inattention.' "

From her room Margalo's voice reached us, sleepy but oozing with self-satisfaction.

"I'm a better girl than the maid," she told us, "I never gave one tiny little moment of inattention all day long."

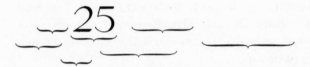

25

SOMETHING felt strange and for the first few minutes after waking I could not discover what it was. I sat up in bed, reassured myself that I felt splendid, focused on objects to test my eyesight, and achieved the melancholy proof it was as good as it had been yesterday and as my age would allow it to be. Nevertheless there was something different around me, or more specifically under me. A lack of firm foundation, and when I had narrowed the feeling down to this I knew what was causing it. We were moving. We had always tied up at night and not started next day until some time after breakfast, since all of us liked to breakfast early. Now at seven-thirty o'clock we were underway and I am sure this was what had wakened me. I have been on more than one Atlantic crossing when the ship's engines have slowed during the night because of fog or whatever necessity. I have wakened on the instant, aware of the change of rhythm, although until the moment of change I would have been in a deep sleep and unaware of the sound or the movement itself of the ship. I would ask Sam to explain to me the basis of communication between the subconscious and a change that is not accompanied by any warning sound.

When I came into the saloon I found the others finishing their breakfast, saw the doors open and on the deck Richard and Jenny setting up beach umbrellas. The General called to me: "What made you so late? Didn't you feel us leave at seven? Everyone else got right up to see what was going on."

My sensory perception was not so extra as I had thought. I saw no reason to admit it.

"Of course," was my answer, "but it was delicious to lie in bed and hear the water lapping." I was not sure I had heard water lap, so to avoid questioning chose an unoccupied table and changed the subject by asking why we had made such an early start.

Everyone was eager to tell me, and to ask me why I was so backward about receiving absorbing information. I considered the question not worth answering.

We were leaving at seven because we must moor that night at Ravières. We must also visit the château at Ancy-le-Franc. If we did not arrive for the eleven-o'clock tour, we would have to wait for the two-o'clock; then we would not reach Ravières.

A pedestrian or bicylist we might have passed on our morning run would not have fancied he saw a speedboat rushing by, but the *Palinurus* urged to her utmost by David did allow us to reach the château by eleven o'clock, when the morning tour began. I doubt the Captain of the *United States* felt prouder after a record crossing than Richard and David over their achievement. At a lope, the instant they docked, we covered the ground between our landing place and the château gates. We were breathless but jubilant when they closed behind us and not in our faces.

Once inside we scattered as usual and, adroitly evading the guide as much as possible, went our separate ways. I dropped behind the tour at the chapel, and happily for me this guide neither hounded nor herded his flock. He was unlike most guides too in another way—and as a group they are anathema to me. He did not confine his information to statistics about the dimensions of each room, the number of tiles in the floor, pieces of glass in a window, stitches in a tapestry and other spellbinding data.

This one told his group, while I was still within hearing, the present owner is the Princesse de Mérode, representing the fifth generation in direct succession to the original owners, the family of Clermont-Tonnerre. Although, he added, reluctantly, the fifth generation was considered a direct succession only by reason of the marriage alliance between the Princesse de Mérode and Clermont-Tonnerre "effected" by the mother of the princess. The effect of their merger—and I thought this an imposing way to identify marriage—had been a happy one for the château, since the Princesse de Mérode, the current owner, took excellent care of the property. Though she lived in Belgium she came to the château several times a year to make sure everything was in order. I conjured up an image of the Princesse arriving for spring and fall cleaning equipped with mops, brooms, pail and cleansing powders but dismissed this as too fanciful. Nevertheless, whatever details the guide may have added beyond my hearing, the guidebook itself says, "Due to this care the interiors have retained their purity and primitive state and the exterior architecture has never submitted to any modification or deterioration."

We were unanimous in our enjoyment of the interior.

(Our pleasure in the furnishings may have been unalloyed because we were suitably dressed and did not meet any ambassadors.)

Aubusson and Beauvais tapestries that cover its walls are as magnificent as the size itself of the guardroom (Salle des Gardes). I stayed longer than the others in the chapel to enjoy with leisure its woodwork of exquisite painted panelings, and the frescoed arches. The subtle color in the Gallery of Sacrifices (Galerie des Sacrifices), I learned from the guidebook, is gray poplar of which the paneling is made. The furniture of the château like the architecture itself is for the most part Italian Renaissance. This makes for an uninterrupted flow of color and design without the jarring anachronisms, in our opinion, of the furnishings at Tanlay.

Frances discovered one flaw and was disturbed by it. I was present almost at the moment of discovery. When I came out of the château she was standing in the outer court looking down at the compass in her hand. I asked if she was getting her bearings. She shook her head. "I thought so," she said. "Now I've proved I'm right and I don't understand it. The château faces north, the servants' quarters have a southern exposure. Nothing around for miles. Why did they choose north? The guidebook does not say why." I left her brooding over the instrument and the enigma.

There was no one on deck when I came aboard, but I heard splashing on the far side and voices that were familiar though I had never heard them so loud. Richard and David were swimming, and as I reached the rail Richard gave a triumphant shout when he tipped David off a rubber mattress. I had seen and heard Richard in high spirits only once before but that was on a night I did not like to remember. This was a joy to watch on a bright sunny day and, for the first time on the cruise, really hot. I watched them with a twinge of envy; but at the moment Richard, catching sight of me, urged me to join them and I was tempted (I had brought a bathing suit), I saw Jenny from the stern empty the trash baskets from the cabins. The temptation evaporated. I know garbage is not emptied into the canal and that on the summer cruises swimming is included in the daily program, but at that moment I did not find the prospect appealing and went below to get ready for lunch.

My cabin was on the quay side and I could hear footsteps on the gangplank. I was speculating idly the possibility of identifying the owner by his tread when I heard a fragment of conversation that stamped an identification: "But we will have to get some money." I knew the Hacketts had come aboard.

Our barge, turned speedboat, brought us to the outskirts of Ravières at four o'clock. With something close to a flourish we nosed into the bank and moored. We had not exceeded the speed limit that is rigidly observed on the canals—because the wash from a vessel must not be allowed to weaken the banks—but we had maintained a spanking pace of four miles an hour.

In the mysterious way that a pattern unplanned takes definite shape when people travel together, one part of ours was that Neill and Sophy retrieved the car each day. It only now occurs to me the reason for this was probably that Neill, from the daily study of maps and guidebooks, would have marked places in the area he wanted to investigate. The General's liking was primarily to drive the car and second to explore the countryside. At Ravières there was a slight deviation in the pattern: Albert and Frances asked if they might accompany Neill and Sophy. When this suggestion had been happily accepted the pattern resumed its established form.

The Hacketts might find a place somewhere, they said, that would cash an Express check. The prospect of such a find was dim, they admitted instantly, forestalling any sentiments of doubt, but, they added, their need was so urgent they must not forego any possibility of rescue. They could not understand how such a situation could have developed; they had completely run out of money.

When the double-daters left, Romney and I were playing a game of Scrabble. I refused his challenge to another and he declined my invitation to go ashore for a walk. I do not know where the others were when I started my walk, but quitting the boat I had seen Romney was conforming to his pattern, and Margalo's. They sat back to back, each engrossed in a private game of solitaire. I walked only about twenty minutes because the day was hot, and I thought how wise we had been to choose these two weeks for our cruise, since this part of the country was already moving into summer weather.

A second thought reminded me wisdom had had nothing to do with our choice. This fortnight was the only available time in the schedule of the *Palinurus*. However, I said to myself—simultaneously aware that I talk to myself frequently and at some length (I am sure it has nothing to do with age; it is only an idiosyncrasy)—so I said to myself if I had the choice of another time, I would choose this very slice of the calendar or perhaps the autumn when the poplars have turned yellow and the fields a softer green.

The land travelers drew up alongside the barge shortly after my return. Before climbing down from the Microbus— and I use the word carefully—you do not step out of a Microbus, you climb down from it, shifting from one support to the next one lower, until the ground is reached—Neill and Sophy checked the time and mileage from the previous night's parking spot at Ancy-le-Libre. Every day it delighted them to compare land distance and time with the progress of the barge. This span could not have been more than ten miles and we had left at 7 A.M. in the morning, but I did not hear the exact computation because Frances and Albert descending were calling out their triumphant jubilation over being in the money again. They did not waste time by coming aboard. They set off immediately on foot.

Margalo, who seldom voices the obvious, called after them, "Postcards?" and Albert looked back grinning and widening his eyes, "Maybe ice cream too."

Margalo, Romney, Cornelia and I had come on deck to welcome the returning motorists. Sam was not with us. Cornelia made a sudden decision to go with the Hacketts and hallooed to them to wait. Although she denies this with indignation and some rancor, I maintain Cornelia's customary gait is of such stateliness it is sometimes feasible to keep an eye on an immovable object to make sure she is passing it. She says in retaliation that at least she doesn't stop to explain, but that I cannot ask the simplest question, order a meal, make a purchase without pausing to include my reasons and usually a considerable portion of family history. This time the patterns were reversed. Because she is a considerate person she did not keep the Hacketts waiting; she hurried. She almost scuttled after them, but halfway there she stopped, turned back to us and *explained*, "I never eat ice cream and I only send postcards to my small grandson, but I want exercise."

Sophy and Neill had not left the car. They were waiting, Neill said, to see if anyone would like to go with them for more exploring of the countryside, it was so beautiful. Margalo declined and went back to her game of solitaire. They knew I would accept—actually they had come back to fetch me because I always wanted to explore the countryside—but when Romney said he would like to come we were surprised and said so.

"I never thought to hear you choose nature over solitaire," was my way of putting it.

"You never will," was his answer as he climbed up the

Microbus, "but I'll always choose people. When Margalo and I play solitaire it's companionable, but it's not a lively exchange of ideas. Shall we talk?"

On my short walk I had gone as far as the bridge spanning the Armançon River that in this part of its course runs companionably along one side of the canal. I suggested we begin our little tour there because the view from the bridge would delight them. It did. The canal, so thickly bordered by trees, tall and very nearly meeting above, was a tunnel of still water, muted green with occasional highlights where the foliage was thin enough to allow the sun to sprinkle dancing polka dots. The river, however, was no tunnel. It was as open as the sky itself; broad meadows on either side were in full sunlight. We came to the little village of Nuits. I find it odd if not sinister that an inhabited place should be named Nights. I can find no legend that gives a reason for it, but even "curiouser" is someone's fondness for the name that has brought its repetition in the neighborhood with appendages to set them apart. This one is called Nuits-sous-Rivières.

Most guidebooks do not mention it; Baedecker says only "a village formerly fortified." There is no evidence now of anything so aggressive as even the ruins of a fortification. I have been permitted by the General to read her diary in order to verify dates and places. She is always accurate; she is never loquacious. Of Nuits she has written, "Crossed the River into Nuits, found it charming." My notes do not include the date when we saw it. They read, "The world I think has gone around Nuits and left it as serene and beautiful as a child asleep." A little florid, I have thought rereading it, and Sophy's a bit stark, but between the two descriptions there emerges an impression of a little place guidebooks need not ignore.

Beyond Nuits after a gentle ride a panorama spread around us so wide we might have been on a mountaintop. I remembered on the road between Pontigny and Brienon we had come to such a spread as this at the crest of a modest hill. When I expressed my satisfaction with this topography and an irritation that it was not more frequently duplicated in other parts of the world without the necessity of mountains, Neill and Romney evidently did not understand, because Sophy amplified:

"Emily hates mountains and mountain roads. When she

has to go on them she keeps her eyes shut so she misses most of the views. You'd never think," she added reflectively, "Emily took a course in geology in college."

"I flunked it," I told them, and suggested we let the topic drop.

Green fields were, of course, striped by yellow mustard and interrupted by silly, gushing brooks hurrying toward the sedate Armançon River. From the number of times we crossed it or caught up alongside, the river was making enough loops and turns to have taught a child how to play Hare and Hounds. I nearly said it was no wonder the land looked and must be so fertile considering the number of streams running through, but I thought better of it. I preferred to veer away from anything related, however remotely, to geology. Instead I drew the attention of the others to a château as we passed it, set at the far end of an avenue of trees but obviously deserted. Sophy obligingly backed the car to the front of the drive so that we could see at leisure the beautiful proportions and façade of the house.

While the two men were discussing its charm Sophy addressed herself to me, though I had not said a word beyond "What a lovely château."

"No," she told me, "it would not be a good idea to see how much it would cost to buy, restore and live in."

"Duke University," I thought to myself bitterly, "ought to engage the General for experiments in ESP," but aloud I told her nothing of the sort had remotely crossed my mind.

It is true the sight of an abandoned house provokes a fantasy that installs me as its châtelaine living graciously, having accomplished a restoration that even exceeds the original beauty of the place. The transfiguration would have to be accomplished by a wave of a wand, since I am so incompetent with my hands I could not make a garden, hammer a nail straight, nor sew, let alone hang a curtain; and almost always

when I have an attack of one of these fantasies I am in posses-
sion of enough wit to realize all my resources expended on
this transfiguration would not even cover it with a new roof.
But a few times, not often in latter years, the fantasy has
crossed the border into reality, and I have been hauled back
by friends in the nick of time from the jaws of man-eating
mortgages and bankruptcy. I can understand how those moments of persuading me to drop the pen that was about to
sign my all away could make my lifesavers nervous, but it is
disconcerting to be checked at the very threshold of only a
fantasy.

We drove on, through a tiny village that seemed to be
approximately one block long and one street wide. At its outskirts we were stopped by the descent of gates at a railroad
crossing of a single track without curves as far as we could
look. The only surprising thing about this unrestricted view
was that there was no train on its horizon coming from either
direction. Romney suggested reasons for checking us. The
guard had just painted the gates—and the shining wooden
barriers, alternately red and white, did justify this speculation—and he was spreading them out to dry. Or there was so
little occasion to use them he exercised the barrier occasionally, in case a train would come along one day. I told him on a
trip in Portugal we had frequently waited at a barrier twenty
minutes or more but a train had come eventually. When that
amount of time had passed and there was still no puff of
smoke in the distance I began to doubt the Portuguese timing would be repeated here.

A herd of cows approached us from the other side of the
barrier. I think I had first noticed them far down the road
when the gates went down. I had thought there would have
to be concessions to each party when we met, but when the
animals came up almost to the railroad gate they turned
into a narrow side lane that veered away from the track. The

herdsman was at the rear, of course, bringing up the stragglers. He may have been eight years old; he looked no more than six. The car windows were open on either side, enabling us to look up and down the track.

I called, "Can you tell us when the train is coming?"

" 'Oh, madame,' he answered, and gave a funny little bow. His eyes were twinkling, but he spoke gravely in a sweet high voice; my heart yearned toward him. 'The gates are for my cows so they will not continue on the road, and go into the village. When the guard sees us coming in the morning and at night he puts them down.' "

"Is there no train at all?" Romney asked.

"Perhaps," we were told with scrupulous accuracy, "but I have not seen one."

"But there is a guard." This was from Neill, who likes to pursue facts.

"Oh yes, monsieur, he has been here a long time, he is very old, there are more cows than mine, you know, he takes care of them all. Now he will lift the gates so you can continue. Bon soir, m'sieur, 'dame."

The gates had lifted but I was not looking. I only knew this when Sophy moved ahead so forcefully I rapped my chin smartly on the window ledge.

Drawing in my head, feeling it a bit gingerly and blinking away involuntary tears, I expostulated.

"I had to get away fast," Sophy defended her convulsive start. "You were about to ask that little boy if he would like to come to America."

It was mortifying to have two of my weaknessess exposed in such rapid succession, but it is true that on various trips abroad in which Sophy has participated I have been moved to invite young people in various countries to come home with me, not groups, but individuals. I accomplished this once with a young girl from Greece, and the success of that transplanting has brought deep contentment to me and to her, living with a husband and four children on Long Island.* I do perhaps suffer a giddiness in the head, from success, and want to do it again, but I do not know what gave Sophy the impression I was visualizing that dear little boy growing up to be a distinguished citizen of the United States. She jarred away the image when my chin smacked the window ledge.

On our way home we passed Sam perhaps a mile from the barge. He was standing on the edge of the road in deep conversation with a peasant woman who wore full-skirted working clothes, kerchief over her head. As we went by we could see her face was browned by the sun, and furrowed by her endeavor to understand what was being said to her.

Romney groaned. "He's asking her to dinner and she is accepting." He paused, ruminating a moment. "She is a midwife," he pronounced. "We will be asked to translate her techniques and those in America. God grant she does not bring her instruments to show," he added fervently.

God granted that she did not come to dinner and she was not a midwife, but Sam told us all about her vocation. Those were her sheep we had seen in the meadow where he had been standing. She took them out very early each morning, brought them home for lunch, hers, and a brief siesta, also hers. She then took them out again until six o'clock in the evening. We no longer asked Sam how he found out these things and were not even surprised when, in answer to a query if he had met anyone else, he said yes indeed he had had a most interesting talk with a rock cutter who is really a sculptor and had given him a large piece of rock he was going to take back to New York. He had also had conversation with two men felling trees and learned a great deal about an ingenious and time-saving method they had devised.

We dined that night—and it was our last—as we had dined on the first evening, with Captain and crew. We would reach

* *Water, Water Everywhere,* and *Forever Old, Forever New.*